FOR THE LOVE OF GOLD

Calvin didn't get a chance to finish because Lester shot him. Not once. The little man was so incensed that he shot his partner three times.

Calvin lay spread-eagled on the rocks, his eyes fixed on the vein of gold. "Give me another big nugget."

"Okay," Bruin said, "but you aren't going to live to spend it."

"I know."

Bruin could see Calvin's eyes beginning to lose focus. "Why did you do it?" he asked, placing a nugget in his fist and unbuttoning his shirt to study the bullet wounds.

"Because I wanted to be rich," Calvin said, blood oozing from the corner of his mouth. "I've always been poor as dirt. I just wanted to be rich one day in my life. Is that so much to ask?"

The man's fingers were trembling but they wrapped themselves around the nugget and squeezed it so fiercely that the tips of his fingers turned white. "How much am I worth right now?"

"At least a thousand dollars and maybe more."

Calvin's eyes sparkled for just an instant and then their light died.

RESTITUTION

Gary McCarthy

BERKLEY BOOKS, NEW YORK

This is a work of fiction. Names, characters, places, and incidents either are the product of the author's imagination or are used fictitiously, and any resemblance to actual persons, living or dead, business establishments, events, or locales is entirely coincidental.

RESTITUTION

A Berkley Book / published by arrangement with the author

PRINTING HISTORY
Berkley edition / December 2003

ISBN: 0-425-19322-5

BERKLEY ®
Berkley Books are published by The Berkley Publishing Group, a division of Penguin Group (USA) Inc.,
375 Hudson Street, New York, New York 10014.
BERKLEY and the "B" design
are trademarks belonging to Penguin Group (USA) Inc.

PRINTED IN THE UNITED STATES OF AMERICA

10 9 8 7 6 5 4 3 2

To my loving wife and best friend,
Jane Henry McCarthy,
and to
Bruin Henry, R.I.P.

PROLOGUE

—⁓—

His name was Bruin Henry, and the first time I saw him ride his Missouri mule into Prescott, I thought he was bigger and more terrible-looking than a grizzly bear. I had never seen a man so scarred and fierce, although I was almost thirteen and believed I had already seen the worst of Arizona Territory's humanity. Our eyes touched only a moment, but it caused a chill to shiver up my spine and my scalp to prickle. I was not the only one who felt that way, for I saw hard frontier men turn aside or drop their eyes like submissive dogs.

I recall that Bruin's wild black hair was streaked with silver and his beard was liberally matted with grease. He wore a buckskin shirt, gray flannel pants, and his gun was hitched up high on the right side, while a bowie knife of prodigious proportions rode on his left. Even his mule seemed bigger than life, and when it passed a hitching rail, that white, mangy beast laid its long ears back and showed a set of yellow teeth. The horses shied away in terror, and one broke free and went racing down Prescott's Whiskey Row.

Bruin's eyes were sunk under thick, bushy brows, and they

had a dark hardness in them like obsidian. He did not turn his head much one way or the other, yet I had a strong sense that he was looking for someone.

How could I have known that Bruin Henry was my murdering outlaw granddaddy and he'd come to Prescott, Arizona, looking for *me*?

ONE

—⚡—

BRUIN HENRY FELT his heart quicken with excitement as he bent low to the hard rock face of a cliff lost deep in the Superstition Mountains. His eyes bulged and he snorted deep in his throat, then raised his miner's pick one more time and struck the granite-and-quartz rock face with a mighty blow. There was what he had been searching for all these many years, a vein of pure gold.

The pick fell forgotten from his huge, calloused hands, and Bruin collapsed to his knees shaking like aspen leaves in a high mountain wind. For several long and breathless moments, the giant could not move, and the thought occurred to him that his heart might fail. If so, he would never die a happier man.

"We're rich," he whispered in a hoarse voice seldom used. He turned to his mule, now watching him with more than normal interest. "Maggot, we're *both* rich!"

The mule was smart, smarter even than most of its kind, and it knew that something very important had just taken place. Never before had it heard its master's voice so filled with joy and jubilation. The beast's enormous ears twitched, and it nuzzled the outlaw-turned-prospector.

"It's a pure vein of gold," Bruin choked out. "It's small to the eye now, but it might get wider and deeper. It runs under this huge boulder, and that's why it's so well hidden. Why, so many others must have passed it by all these years. But we found it, Maggot! We found it and now we're going to be rich and happy! You're going to have oats to eat, and I'll have whiskey and steaks whenever I want, and we'll do all those things that we've talked about so many years. Yes, sir, we'll make up for lost time and we'll set things right by changin' the wrongs that I've done. I swear I will make my amends."

Bruin Henry turned his face up to the clear, blue sky. He pushed back his sweat-stained excuse for a Stetson, and then raised his hands upward in a gesture of supplication. "Lord, I was a wicked, wicked man. In my younger days, I sinned in all ways possible. I have robbed and cussed and fornicated. I have lied and cheated and stolen most any damned thing I could lay my paws upon and which would bring me a lousy dollar. And most of all, I have lost my wife and the love and respect of my daughter, sweet Kate."

Tears welled up in his eyes and ran freely into his bushy beard. "For seventeen years, I have wandered alone in the wilderness. Avoiding decent men and virtuous women for fear that my terrible temper and evil nature might overcome my good intentions. But now, Lord, you have blessed me and Maggot with this vein of gold and shown me that I am *not* beyond redemption!"

Bruin covered his sun-blistered face and wept so passionately that his body heaved as if he had taken a deadly dose of poison. The white mule grew afraid, and it raised its head and hee-hawed at the desolate mountains.

AFTER DISCOVERING THE gold, Bruin worked three more days, and wept many times because the vein was as rich as he had dared to dream. But on the fourth day, he saw a thin spiral of smoke and knew that other prospectors were nearby. His joy suddenly turned to dread, and he worked frantically to cover up the vein and all evidence of its uncovering. He would have liked to have rolled the great boulder tighter over the thin crevasse of quartz that had only recently been revealed by a sudden flood. Quartz was often a certain giveaway for the presence of gold, and now he would have to rebury the shiny crystals or his discovery would certainly be found.

The Superstition Mountains were crawling with men like himself seeking buried treasure. Most were fools who believed in Spanish gold hidden by the explorers, or else bounty stashed by stagecoach robbers who often fled to this wilderness with a posse close on their heels. In fact, it was the ruggedness and savagery of these mountains that had long given refuge to outlaws and raiding Apache.

"What can I do now?" he asked himself as he frantically covered every shred of his discovery. "If I stay here, they will find me and know that I have discovered gold. Killers will come and I will never be able to fight them all off. They will kill me . . . and you too, Maggot . . . and then they will steal our gold!"

Bruin Henry shook his head, feeling suddenly overwhelmed by the responsibility of being rich and having lived such a bad life. This was his last and only chance to make amends, but that certainly did not mean he could kill even more men despite their thieving intentions.

"Maggot," he said, "there is only one thing we can do, and that is to stake this claim and then hire men to protect it while I mine out the vein."

The mule heard reason and calmness return to its master's gravelly voice. It flicked its ears in agreement.

"Let's break camp and get out of here fast," Bruin said, grabbing up his rifle and gun before scurrying down the hillside to his bedroll and provisions.

"We'll stake the claim in Prescott and I'll hire a few hon-

est men to bring back here. But can honest men be found?
Can we trust anyone?"

Bruin Henry shook his head, for he did not believe there
was anyone in this territory honest enough to hire. But he
would try. He would do everything within his power to bring
his fortune back to civilization and then to use it for good.

He saddled the mule and loaded his saddlebags with a few
cans of beans and a tobacco can filled with gleaming nuggets.

How far was it to Prescott? Bruin guessed it would take at
least five days to reach the territorial capital and stake a legal
mining claim. Then another three days to hire a few men, and
five more days to return.

Thirteen days!

Bruin pulled at his beard, and a deep frown creased his
brow as he mounted his Missouri mule. "Thirteen days," he
said, taking a final look back at the face of the cliff. *Maggot,
I hate to tell you this, and I know the Lord doesn't approve of
being superstitious, but thirteen is a very unlucky number. I
was thirteen when I had to kill Uncle Luther for messin' with
my little cousin Josey. And it was the thirteenth day of July
twenty years ago when I charged up that hill in Virginia and
killed four Johnny Rebs . . . the last one wounded and begging for his life. And finally, it was January 13 when I committed my last stagecoach robbery and my murdering
son-in-law, Link Cochran, executed four passengers before I
could react fast enough to stop him and keep the driver and
guard from being killed.*

Bruin Henry urged his mule into a trot and pulled his rifle
from its scabbard. Three days ago he had thought himself the
luckiest man on earth. But now, superstitious fool that he was,
Bruin felt almost cursed.

Good things came, but they were always followed by bad.
Bruin knew this to be as true as night following day because
he had lost every good thing that he'd ever had in his life. And
now he was going back among people. People who might yet
remember that he had been a killer and stagecoach robber
with an as-yet-unclaimed bounty on his head.

For just one moment, Bruin considered forgetting about the gold he'd just found. Maybe he was better off remaining poor and alone, a man with a violent past and no realistic hope for a future. But then he remembered his red-haired daughter Kate and his granddaughter, Ophelia. It had been so long since he'd seen them, and maybe . . . maybe now he could ask them for forgiveness and make their lives easier with his gold.

And if forgiveness wasn't in their hearts, the very least he could do was to stake his claim and use his newfound wealth for the good of the others he'd wronged. If he was shot or hanged for taking that risk, well, at least he would have left this world with the best of intentions.

TWO

—◆—

Two DAYS LATER, Bruin awoke in the night feeling that something was wrong. His campfire was almost extinguished, no more than a bed of ash and coals. High overhead, the moon was lurking behind clouds so that he could barely see Maggot tethered only a few yards away.

"Somethin' wrong?" he said in a soft voice. "Cougar or bear got you spooked?"

The mule was restless and stomping its hooves. Normally, it was a quiet and composed animal, but it greatly feared both the cougar and the black bears that were commonplace in these wild mountains.

Bruin rolled out of his bedroll and found his rifle. He came to his stocking feet and tiptoed over to Maggot. "Don't worry. I'll build up the fire and then nothin' will bother you."

He placed the rifle beside his bedroll and groped around under the pines until he found a small stack of wood that he had gathered. It was his habit to keep enough tinder and twigs to renew his fire for an early morning cup of coffee. Bruin blew softly on the ash and fed the heat into flames. Soon, he had a good fire, but with the mule still fussing over the threat of a cougar or bear, he needed more kindling.

"Dammit, Maggot, it's kinda dark to go pokin' around out there, and I don't want to run into whatever is botherin' you, but I'll find a branch or two," he muttered. "It's a sad thing, the trouble you cause me. I'm too old and stiff to be messin' around in the night."

Bruin was irritated, but the mule had been hard-worked these past two days, so he figured it had earned the right to its own peace of mind. And besides, it didn't take but a couple of minutes of stumbling around in the dark before he had enough wood to heighten the flames and drive away any hungry predators.

"There," he said finally, kneeling beside the fire and squinting out into the black forest. "Now you settle down, Mule."

But despite the fire, Maggot was still unhappy. This bothered Bruin, for he appreciated the animal's intelligence. "What is wrong?" he asked, starting to retrieve his rifle.

His hand never quite reached the weapon. Flashes of gunpowder winked in the night, and Bruin felt as though he had been stuck by lightning. He was knocked into his campfire, and the rifle clattered against rocks as he tried to bat out the flames.

"We got him!" a man shouted.

"Don't kill him. I told you to shoot low!"

"He's afire!" a third man shouted. "I kin smell him burning alive."

Bruin could smell himself burning. His beard was smoldering, and so was his shirt. Not yet in flame, but smoking and burning just the same. He tried to decide if he should raise his hand and bat out fire in his beard, or try to grab the rifle, but he'd been shot twice, and it turned out that neither choice was his to make.

Strong hands dragged him from the campfire ring, and Bruin grabbed one man's wrist and twisted it so hard that it broke.

The man's scream was as high-pitched as that of a woman, and then he sobbed, "He broke my arm!"

"I'll break our neck too if I can get ahold of it!"

The light was still poor, but there was enough for Bruin to see and feel a man standing over him using his boots. One kick to the side of his head nearly put him under, and Bruin heard the man growl, "You better be still or I'll boot your damn head off."

"What do you want with me?" Bruin asked, trying not to lose consciousness.

"You're Bruin Henry and still worth some bounty money down in Yuma. We've been tracking you for weeks. You're a sly one, Bruin Henry."

Bruin started to say something else, but the man whose wrist he'd snapped like a dry twig ran up and kicked him in the jaw. Bruin didn't remember anything after that as he tumbled into a deep, black abyss.

WHEN HE AWOKE, someone was trying to force water down his gullet. Bruin didn't want to awaken. He remembered that there was trouble and pain waiting, so he kept his eyes shut for several minutes, pretending to be unconscious as someone tried to pry open his jaws. When he began to choke, Bruin struggled, but his effort was feeble and his arms and legs were soon pinned.

"So there's still some fight in the old bear," one of the men, a thin fellow with a weasel face and hooked nose, chortled. "He must have been a hell of a man when he was young."

Bruin spat at the weasel's face, and got his nose bloodied. Not that it mattered anymore. His nose had been broken at least six times in fights, but it still hurt. Bruin could taste blood mixing with the water in this throat, and he turned his head aside and vomited.

"You're done for, old man."

He suddenly realized that he *had* to gather his wits or they would kill him as quick as they might swat a fly, and with no more compassion. His voice sounded strange when he shouted with all the false indignation he could muster, "Dammit, I ain't Bruin Henry!"

The weasel drew a gun and pressed its barrel into his ear. "Say that again and I'll blow your brains all over the ground."

"All right, I am Bruin Henry the stagecoach robber."

"Of course you are, and the reward on your head still stands after all these years."

"How much am I still worth?"

"It's gone down to a hundred dollars."

Bruin's mind felt as if it were mired in quicksand, but he managed to think well enough to blurt out, "I . . . I might be able to pay you that much."

They laughed.

Their laughter was galling. "What's so damn funny?"

"What's funny is that your big Missouri mule and rifle are worth nearly a hundred dollars. Besides, the reward says you are worth the money delivered to Yuma alive . . . or dead."

Dead or alive? Why, if he'd have been them, he'd have killed Bruin Henry too.

One of the men, a bat-eared fellow with buck teeth, leaned close and raised Bruin's knife up before his eyes. "Big man who once wore a great big knife," he said softly, ominously. "I think I'll slit your throat right now and then hack off your head, then I'll deliver it to Yuma in a canvas bag and dump it on the marshal's desk."

The third one was the smallest, and he looked crazy with his eyes rolling around like lead balls in a bucket. It was his wrist that Bruin had broken, and now it was bound up with strips of leather. He crowed, "Boys, can you imagine the look on the marshal's face when he sees old Bruin's head rollin' around on his desk! Why, I bet he'll piss his pants."

"Soil 'em too," the weasel-faced one said, narrow shoulders rocking with pent-up laughter. "It's gonna be a sight for certain! We'll be celebrities down in Yuma. Heroes!"

"And then we'll head for old Mexico and the tequila and get us some lovin' from them pretty little women!"

Bruin stared up into the pitiless gaze of the man who held a blade at his throat. It was like looking into the eyes of a feral animal.

"Say your prayers," the man hissed with a cruel smile.

Bruin recalled how sharp he kept his knife, and knew that he didn't have a ghost of a chance to keep this devil from slitting his throat. The huge bowie knife would slice through his jugular and windpipe as easily as if they were warm butter.

"Wait!" he choked. "I can pay you a thousand!"

The knife had already split his skin, and Bruin could feel a rivulet of warm blood, but his words gave the man pause. "A *thousand* dollars?"

"That's right." Bruin almost nodded his head, and that would have been fatal.

"Where are you gonna get *that* kind of money?"

"Why, from all the stagecoaches I robbed. I spent some, but the rest I stashed here and there."

Bruin was a terrible liar, and his words rang hollow even to himself. The truth was he'd long since spent all of his stagecoach robbery money, and had nothing left to show for his lawless days except a guilty conscience.

"You're a damn liar."

Bruin decided he had better change his tactics if he wanted to keep on breathing. "Okay, boys, I can't fool you. The truth of is that I spent all my stolen money years ago. But I do have a hidden gold mine that's worth a small fortune. In fact, I was on my way over to Prescott to file a claim when you caught me off guard."

"Gold?"

"That's right."

Bruin saw a flicker of interest and maybe even excitement in their cold eyes.

The man with his knife licked his thin lips. "Bruin, how long have you been prospecting in the Superstitions?"

"Seventeen years."

"So where is this gold discovery?"

Bruin chose his next words carefully. If he told them it was far away, they'd know he was lying again. However, he did need precious time to figure out how to escape, so he said, "Not so far away."

The weasel-faced one howled, "Oh, bullshit! If you had gold, you sure wouldn't be out here grubbing around in these mountains."

The knife started to press back down on his throat, and Bruin shouted, "What good would gold do me if I went to a town and was arrested and hanged?"

"I still say he's lyin'!" the crazy-eyed man yelled. "Tom, cut his throat or I'll do it myself."

"Wait," Bruin yelled. "I can *prove* it I have a gold mine. There are nuggets in my pack."

"Lester, Calvin, go see if he's tellin' us the truth!" Tom ordered his companions. Then, looking down at Bruin, he hissed, "If there ain't no gold, you're gonna die slow."

"There's gold," Bruin said with cold sweat drenching his body. "There's probably five hundred dollars worth. And there's plenty more where that came from."

Long minutes passed, and Bruin closed his eyes waiting for his precious gold nuggets to be found. Nuggets he'd need to hire men and buy supplies so that he could return and extract his waiting fortune. And while he suspected that the greed of these men would now insure he'd live a little longer, that didn't change his unlucky circumstances. One thing he did vow was that, even if it cost him his life, he would never tell them the true location of his recent gold discovery. Not only because he was beginning to hate them, but because they'd kill him for certain.

"We found it!" Calvin shouted. "By damned, we're gonna be rich!"

Tom was so excited he sprang to his feet. If he was thinking at all, he must have thought that Bruin was in no condition to move, much less offer a fight. But he was wrong. Bruin kicked out his good leg and knocked Tom flying. He rolled, grabbed a rock from his fire ring, and with his good arm, he hurled it straight and hard.

The rock struck Tom right between his feral eyes and knocked him down kicking and thrashing. Bruin lunged, desperate to grab the fallen man's gun, but Calvin and Lester were too quick and when they landed on him, he hadn't the strength to beat them off. The bat-eared one grabbed Bruin's singed beard and slammed his head up and down until he again lost consciousness.

COLD WATER WAS thrown in Bruin's face. "Wake up. Your bullet wounds ain't bad. We bandaged 'em up so you won't bleed anymore, and now you're taking us to your gold mine."

Bruin was dragged to his feet. His eyes came to rest on Tom, and he realized the man was dead.

"Exactly how far is it to your mine?"

"Twenty miles. Maybe a couple more or less."

"Your mule is saddled. Mount up."

Bruin glanced over at the man he'd killed with a rock. Tom's eyes were staring up at the sun, but the only thing he was seeing was eternity. Bruin turned back to the other pair. "Ain't you even going to bury your friend?"

"Let the vultures pick his bones," Lester said, breaking into wild laughter and rolling his crazy eyes. "He'd have done the same for us if we'd have died. Ain't that right, Calvin?"

"He sure would have," Calvin agreed. "Mount up, Henry. If you try to run away, we'll blow a hole in your back big enough for a damn rat to crawl through."

"Yeah," the other added, "and then we'll kill and roast your white mule."

"No, you won't," Bruin said, wanting to attack, but knowing this wasn't the time or place. "He's too valuable to eat."

Lester spat in the dirt. "Bruin Henry, I don't like you."

"Well, I don't like you much either," Bruin said, realizing the ridiculousness of this exchange, but prodding the smaller man anyway. "And if it was just you and me, I'd wring your scrawny neck."

It was a stupid thing to say, and it almost earned him a bullet. Fortunately, Calvin jumped between them and said, "Lester, you fool, he's our chance to finally be rich. Put your gun away!"

The small man shook all over, but had just enough reason to see that his partner was right. "Well . . . well," he sputtered in a rage, "then I'll put a bullet in his mule."

Bruin almost knocked Calvin aside in his own anger, and he growled, "If you kill my mule, you're gonna have to kill me too."

Lester must have thought that was a fine idea because he tried to drag his gun from its holster, but Calvin slapped him in the face so hard he staggered. "Lester," he shouted, turning his six-gun on his crazy partner, "I told you to leave the mule be!"

"Why!"

"Because, like Henry says, it's valuable."

Calvin waited until Lester whirled and marched away. Then he turned to Bruin and said, "If you take us to your gold we'll let you and the mule live."

"Can I count on that?" Bruin asked, knowing he could not.

"Yeah," Calvin assured him, "because there's honor among thieves."

It was all Bruin could do not to laugh with sarcasm. Instead, he nodded his head and tried to sound beaten but ever hopeful. "I can always find more gold, but I don't want to die. All I ask is just to be set free with my mule."

"You will be," Calvin promised. "Just don't try to do anything."

"I won't," Bruin told the man, trying to look as if he was beaten and defeated.

The way things stood, Bruin figured his only chance was to buy the time and opportunity to catch this pair off guard. When that moment came, despite his wounds, he'd have to act fast and hit them hard. If he failed, he'd be a dead man, but at least he'd go down fighting.

THREE

—m—

"HOW MUCH FARTHER?" Lester whined. "My wrist is killing me! I need whiskey and a doctor!"

"We'll get you both as soon as we can," Calvin assured his partner. "Just bear up to the pain like a man and let's first get to Henry's gold. After that, we'll be rich enough to buy all the whiskey we'll ever want to drink."

"And you'll set me and my mule free," Bruin reminded them. "Yeah," Calvin said, twisting around in his saddle and offering a weak smile. "We'll set you free just like we promised."

"That's all I ask," Bruin said meekly.

Lester was riding drag, and he hissed, "Old man, I owe you for this wrist. And someday, I'll have the satisfaction of making you pay."

"Lester, shut up!" Calvin ordered.

They were riding single-file along a narrow trail that was carrying them along a mountainside. It wasn't more than a game trail, and the brush and trees crowded them on both sides. They hadn't tied Bruin's hands behind his back or his feet together under Maggot's belly, but Calvin did have the mule tethered to a lead rope wrapped around his saddle horn.

Bruin had been forced to lead them toward his new discovery because they had followed his tracks. During the first few hours of riding, he'd decided that his best chance was to push them on and on until they grew tired. The only problem with his plan was that he was also growing tired and weaker. His wounds weren't bleeding, but the vicious kicks and punches he'd taken had exacted their physical toll. So much so that there were times when he actually fell asleep, and then suddenly jerked back awake silently cussing his weakness.

I have to be strong, he kept thinking. *I have to be stronger than Calvin and Lester even though I'm hurt and older. Time is the only friend I have right now except for myself and Maggot.*

"Calvin, we gotta eat and rest for a while," Lester wailed. "I need something to eat. I'm getting shaky!"

"All right. There's a stream up ahead. Ain't that right, Bruin?"

"That's right."

"We can rest there a while, then push on for a few more hours before dark. We've come at least ten miles. Can't be far to go in the morning. Ain't that true?"

Bruin nodded. "We'll come to my claim in the early afternoon."

"How much gold can we expect to get?"

"Depends. The vein might run deep, but it might not. There's no way to tell until we work out the vein."

"But you *think* it runs deep, don't you?" Calvin asked in an earnest voice. "I mean, you been prospecting all these years so you must have some idea about how rich it is."

"Oh," Bruin said, wanting to feed the man's hunger for wealth, "it's plenty rich. I'd guess it's worth at least ten or twenty thousand dollars."

Calvin whistled through his teeth, and his voice betrayed his excitement. "Tell you what, old man. You help us get the gold out, and maybe we'll even let you have some when we turn you loose."

"Like hell we will!" Lester angrily protested. "If you want to give him gold, then do it out of your share . . . not mine."

"Lester, shut up!"

"I ain't gonna shut up!" the suffering man screeched, his face turning purple with rage. "Calvin, I'm tired of you bossing me around all the time! I ain't gonna take it no more."

Bruin was staring at Calvin, and he saw the bat-eared man's eyes flash. "Lester, one of these days I'm going to have my fill of you, and then you'll be sorry. If it weren't for me, you'd be dead by now."

"Well, if it wasn't for me," Lester shot back, "you'd be dead too!"

Calvin twisted back around in the saddle. Bruin could still hear him muttering and cussing. It was clear that Lester was a fool, and that Calvin was the smarter, tougher man. It was equally clear that Calvin was getting fed up with his companion's stupidity and back talk.

Bruin leaned forward in his saddle and patted Maggot on the neck, wanting to let the mule know that there were increasing indications of hope, while thinking, *Maybe I can play one of these men against the other.*

When they reached the stream and let their mounts drink their fill, they dismounted. Bruin was shocked and dismayed to find that he was so wobbly that he had to hang onto his saddle to support his legs. How was he ever going to overcome this pair if he were so unsteady?

"You gonna make it?" Calvin asked as Lester rode on a ways before dismounting.

"I've lost a good deal of blood and I'm no longer a young man."

"Yeah, I can see that," Calvin said. "But I don't know what to tell you and Lester. There's sure no doctors in this country, and moving on is all that we can do."

"I know," Bruin grunted, releasing his grip on the saddle horn and then taking a few shaky steps over to the base of a pine before easing himself to the ground. "I'll hold up. I may be old, but I'm tough."

"Of course you are," Calvin said. "You killed Tom and broke Lester's wrist. With a little more luck, you'd have killed all three of us."

"Luck didn't have anything to do with it," Bruin told his captor. "I wasn't paying attention to my back trail. I got so excited about finding gold that I forgot to be careful."

It was the first true thing he'd said to either man, and Bruin heard the bitterness in his own voice.

"Ah," Calvin said, sitting down close but not near enough to suddenly grab. "You shouldn't be so hard on yourself."

"Why not?"

"Because we all make mistakes."

"Like you did when you saved Lester's life?"

Calvin stared at him, then smiled. "You thinking that you can get us to fight each other so you can escape? That's what you're thinking, isn't it, Henry?"

"It's just obvious that you don't like each other very much. You know what I think?"

Calvin sighed. "No. Tell me."

"You're not going to want to hear this."

"Spit it out!"

"I think you've pushed Lester past his limits. And I have a hunch that, when you and him ride away with my gold, he's going to kill you the very first chance that he gets."

Calvin snorted with derision. "Oh, you *are* a clever one!"

"I don't know about that, but I do know men, and Lester *will* try to kill you."

"No, he won't because he's afraid of me."

"You kick a cowering dog long enough and, sooner or later, it will bite back."

Calvin frowned. "What you say might well be true, but then again, it might not be. What I do know for a fact is that you'd kill me in an instant if I let down my guard. Am I right?"

"I'm not sure of that myself. But if I decide that you're a

man of your word and I'll go free, I expect I'll play out my cards as they fall."

The man climbed to his feet and moved even farther away before he sat down. "How many men besides Tom have you killed in your lifetime?"

"I've only killed the ones that needed killing."

"That's not true. You and Link Cochran gunned down a stagecoach full of passengers."

"I didn't shoot them. Link did."

"Sure," Calvin taunted. "And you just sat on your horse and laughed!"

Bruin could feel his rising anger. He closed his eyes, but that was a mistake because the image of that long-ago day gone all wrong came back to him so vividly that he could hear the screams and smell the gun smoke. Then he saw the bodies and blood. After that, he opened his eyes and found he was breathing hard as he always did when he had those memories.

"I was on the other side of the stagecoach when it happened," he said, more to himself than to Calvin. "I had ordered the driver and the shotgun guard to climb down from their seat, and they did. I was on one side of the stage, Link and the passengers were on the other. Besides keeping a gun on the guard and driver, I was having trouble with the horses. They were spooked and trying to break loose of my hand and run away. While I was fighting with them and trying to watch the guard and the driver, Link gunned the passengers down. It was never supposed to happen that way."

Calvin shook his head in disbelief. "That's your story. Next, you're going to tell me that your friend—"

"Link Cochran was never my friend!"

"Your son-in-law then," Calvin said dismissively. "What about the guard and driver that were killed?"

"I admit that I shot the guard. When the shooting started on the other side of the stagecoach, the guard jumped for his shotgun and I had to kill him or he'd have blown me in half."

"And the driver?"

Bruin ran his thick fingers over his eyes, and his voice was filled with something very close to agony when he whispered, "The fool made the mistake of running around to the other side, where Link shot him in the back."

Calvin shrugged. "It don't matter anymore what really happened. You and Cochran robbed a stagecoach just eight miles east of Yuma, and when the smoke cleared, six men were dead. Either way, you and Link Cochran killed a bunch of innocent people and are murderers."

"That's right," Bruin spat as if the words were acid in his throat. "We're *both* murderers and deserve to be hanged."

"That's what they'll do to you if I take you to Yuma for the reward," Calvin said matter-of-factly. "But I promised you I'd let you go free once Lester and me had your gold."

"That's right," Bruin said. "You promised."

"I'm a man of my word," Calvin said. "And you had better not forget that because I'm your only chance. If you kill me first, Lester will kill you . . . gold or no gold. He's as crazy as a rabid dog and ten times more dangerous."

"So I've noticed."

"But I'm not crazy. I want to be rich."

"We all do."

"Well," Calvin said, "maybe I'll let you keep a saddlebag of gold if you don't give me any trouble and do what you're told."

"That would be good."

Calvin nodded. "Like I told you before, I am a man of my word and am always fair to those that don't cross me."

"I believe you," Bruin said . . . wondering.

It was mid-afternoon the following day when Bruin saw the place where he had discovered the vein of pure gold. They had come out of a stand of pine, and there was the trail and the big boulder. His heart began thumping faster, and Bruin fretted that he might have left some tell-tale sign that would betray his treasure. But Calvin rode past the boulder as if it didn't exist, and then Bruin was past and so was Lester.

So what happens now? Bruin asked himself as they continued on past the fortune in gold. *How much farther can I string this along before Calvin or Lester loses patience and things get ugly? Before they drag me off Maggot and put a gun to my head and pull the trigger?*

"How much farther?" Lester shouted. "I'm running out of patience and I'm about to shoot you in the back!"

Brain heard the smaller man cock the hammer of his pistol, and he stiffened, expecting a bullet. When it didn't come, he yelled, "All right, boys, we're here!"

"We are?" Calvin asked, reining his horse around and looking in every direction as if he expected the ore to be glittering in the bright afternoon sun. "Where's the gold!"

Bruin figured that he might as well show them the vein of pure gold. Maybe they'd want to keep him alive so that he could work the new discovery. One thing sure, they weren't prospectors and wouldn't know how. After that, he'd either be killed, or Calvin would keep his word, give him a stake, and set him and Maggot free. This decision didn't set well, yet Bruin could see no use in going on for another hour or two and then having to face the anger of both deceived men. If that happened, Calvin just might let his crazy partner pull the trigger.

"It's the gold," Bruin announced as he stiffly dismounted. "It's hidden just behind that big boulder. I covered it up so no one else would find it while I went to file my claim in Prescott."

"You sure did a good job," Calvin said, searching for some indication that the site had been prospected. "I don't see a thing."

"Well, it's there," Bruin assured the man. "And if you want me to expose it, I need my rock pick."

Calvin had confiscated it along with his rifle and tied both to his saddle. Now, he untied the pick and dismounted, warning, "Don't try to swing this at my head, old-timer. Lester may be crazy, but he shoots straight and fast."

"I'll try to remember that."

Both men watched as Bruin wrapped his huge hands on the pick and planted his feet on solid ground. With his battered ribs and head, he only took a couple of swings before he got dizzy and weak on his feet and had to lean against the rock for support. The world was spinning around and around and he felt sick to his stomach.

"You okay?" Calvin asked.

"Hell, no, I'm not okay! You and your friend almost killed me."

"Well," Calvin said pointedly, "you shouldn't have put up such a hard fight. Besides, you *did* kill Tom. Here, let me have a try with the pick."

"You ever swung a miner's pick?"

"No, but I've chopped one hell of a lot of firewood, and it can't be that much different."

Had he been in decent condition, Bruin would have chosen that moment to swing the pick at Calvin, then jump behind the boulder and take his chances with Lester. But he simply wasn't up to the deed, so he gave the man his pick and pointed out exactly where to strike.

Minutes later, all of them were staring at the vein of soft yellow gold.

"My, oh, my!" Calvin whispered reverently. "I've been waiting all my life for this moment."

"Yeah, well so did I," Bruin groused. "The difference between us is that I have been prospecting for seventeen years and deserve the gold. You and Lester, on the other hand . . . don't."

"Calvin, knock loose a nugget the size of your fist and give it to me!" Lester cried.

"All right."

Bruin watched the bigger man bring the pick down hard twice, and he dislodged a huge nugget. Bruin was impressed. "Calvin," he said, "those were a couple of good swings. Maybe you missed your true calling."

The man chuckled and beamed with happiness. "Maybe I did at that."

"Give that big nugget to me right now!" Lester screamed.

"No," Calvin said, turning it over and over in his hands and thinking hard. "This one is for Bruin Henry."

Bruin about fell over, and certainly would have if not for the fact that he was leaning hard on the boulder. "What did you just say?" he dared to ask.

Calvin came over and placed the nugget in Bruin's hand. "Get on your mule and ride before I have a change of heart."

Bruin could not believe what he was hearing. "Are you going to shoot me in the back when I start off?"

"Nope. I could let Lester shoot you right now. I told you that I was a man of my word, and I am. So take the nugget and get out of here fast before we change our minds."

Bruin swallowed hard, and although he was being robbed of a fortune, he was filled with such gratitude that he heard himself actually say, "Thanks."

"Get out of here!"

"Calvin!" Lester cried as Bruin struggled back onto the mule. "Calvin, we ain't gonna let him get away. Not really, are we?"

"Lester, there's a lot more like the nugget I just gave the man. He made us both rich, and besides, I gave him my word."

"Well, I damn sure didn't!"

"It's just one nugget, Lester. Let him—"

Calvin didn't get a chance to finish because Lester shot him. Not once. The little man was so incensed that he shot his partner three times.

With gunfire in his ears, Bruin whipped Maggot forward, and the huge mule ran right over Lester. Maybe the mule broke the small man's remaining good arm, or perhaps he dislocated Lester's shoulder. Either way, the crazy bastard was hurt and struggling to get his gun aimed at Bruin when Maggot ran him down a second time.

Bruin threw himself off the mule and fell hard. He grabbed the six-gun from Lester's hand and emptied it into his chest. "Calvin!"

The man lay spread-eagled on the rocks, his eyes fixed on the vein of gold. "Give me another big nugget."

"Okay," Bruin said, "but you aren't going to live to spend it."

"I know."

Bruin knelt beside the man. He could see Calvin's eyes beginning to lose focus. "Why did you do it?" he asked, placing a nugget in his fist and unbuttoning his shirt to study the bullet wounds.

"Because I wanted to be rich," Calvin said, blood oozing from the corner of his mouth. "I've always been poor as dirt. I just wanted to be rich one day in my life. Is that so much to ask?"

"I never thought so."

"Me neither. I'm an educated man, you know. I should have been a banker or owned a big mercantile or something like that. But I made some bad mistakes when I was young and . . . well, you know how it can go all wrong and how you can't turn things around the right way."

"Yeah, I know," Bruin said. "One terrible mistake can ruin all your chances. But, Calvin, you're rich right now. I just put a huge old nugget in your hand."

Calvin tried to raise it up before his eyes, but his strength was bleeding away so quickly, he grunted and shook and failed.

"Here," Bruin said, helping the man out.

The man's fingers were trembling but they wrapped themselves around the nugget and squeezed it so fiercely that the tips of his fingers turned white. "How much am I worth right now?"

"At least a thousand dollars and maybe more."

Calvin's eyes sparkled for just an instant, and then their light died.

FOUR

———ᨃ———

Bʀᴜɪɴ ʙᴜʀɪᴇᴅ ᴄᴀʟᴠɪɴ up in the trees, but all he did with Lester's body was to let Maggot drag it about a mile down the mountainside where it would never be found. He carefully buried his claim, then rested and recuperated from his injuries for three more days. His bullet wounds had never been life-threatening, but they did need cleaning and some time to heal. He walked with a limp, but that would pass, and the ringing in his ears began to grow dimmer with each passing day.

Bruin would have liked to have made a camp near a beautiful spring he knew existed not far away, and rested even longer, but after his close call he felt a renewed urgency to file his mining claim in Prescott. More than ever, he was afraid someone else would show up unexpectedly, or decide to follow his tracks just like Tom, Calvin, and Lester.

Calvin's death had left him feeling melancholy. He'd never believed the man would let him live, much less have any gold, until that final moment before Calvin was shot.

"I guess I can't read men as well as I used to," he told Maggot. "Was a time when I could tell if a man was telling

me the truth or a lie . . . but not anymore. I wish Calvin had
lived. Maybe he and I could have become friends and
prospected together. Two men who messed up their lives early
and then never quite got 'em back on track. I just wish I had
been able to save Calvin, and failing that, knew if he had a
family that I could visit and at least tell 'em that he was a man
of his word to the very end."

The biggest and most perplexing problem Bruin had was
in trying to decide what to do with the three men's outfits. He
couldn't stand the idea of just burying everything up in the
forest and letting it rot. Why, hellfire, their horses, saddles,
pistols, and rifles alone were worth hundreds of dollars. More
money than he'd made prospecting in most years.

You've been way too poor way too long, he told himself. *If
you take their horses and gear to Prescott, someone might
recognize 'em and, even if they didn't, it would be unusual
enough that it would attract a lot of unwanted attention.
You'll get attention enough there, Bruin Henry. So figure out
how to get rid of the horses and gear and avoid yourself extra
trouble. Besides, with your new gold discovery you don't need
to worry about money.*

Having made his decision, Bruin led Tom, Calvin, and
Lester's horses about twenty miles, and then unsaddled the
animals deep in a rough box canyon and hid their outfits in a
small cave. He drove the three horses out of the canyon and
scattered them in all directions. Finally, he spent a few hours
using a mesquite branch to wipe out his tracks. With sweat
leaking down his spine from his hard exertion, Bruin felt
pretty sure that no one would be able to discover his hidden
cache. Given that the three men's saddles, weapons, and gear
were well hidden in the back of this remote cave, he figured
it might be years before they were discovered.

"Goes back to my outlaw days when I used to hide water,
food, extra bullets, and rifles," he explained to Maggot. "A
man on the run, even an old one like myself, needs to have a
good hiding place where he can replenish his needs if he's
being chased by a posse. If my luck ever turns real sour, sell-

ing those outfits might be enough to save my hide or at least to give us another grubstake."

HIS TRIP OVER to the territorial capital was uneventful. Bruin had crossed the Salt River, now low with many wide sandbars, then traveled northwest to the Verde River, which he very much favored. The air had been hot down in the low country, but it began to cool as he and Maggot traveled up the Verde Valley, already being homesteaded by ranchers and farmers. They came upon the Agua Fria River, and lingered one extra day camping in the cottonwoods. Bruin found a trader and bought extra bullets for Calvin's big-bored buffalo rifle, and then he continued on up into the Prescott Valley, where the air was sweet with the scent of pine forests and the grass was long and green.

"A whole lot more homesteaders up here than when we came through this country four or five years ago," he said, more to himself than the mule. "Still a handsome country, though."

Despite his apprehension about being recognized because of his huge size, Bruin realized he was feeling pretty good. And why not? He had managed to survive three men, and on top of that, he was now rich. Finally, after all the years, he'd have a chance to make some amends . . . provided he wasn't arrested. And that seemed highly unlikely. They might have an old and yellowing wanted poster with a poor drawing of his mug at the marshal's office in Yuma, but he sure doubted that they'd have one up in the northern part of the territory.

He and the huge Missouri mule attracted more and more attention as they drew within sight of the Arizona's fledgling capital. Attention wasn't what Bruin wanted or needed, but because of his size and fierce appearance, he wasn't surprised. Also, there weren't many mules as big or as ugly as Maggot, who never failed to garner at least a second glance.

"I have always liked Prescott," he announced to the mule as the town grew closer. "Last time I saw my daughter was right here in Prescott. I tried to talk to her, but Kate wouldn't even speak to me because of the stagecoach killings."

Bruin shook his head, almost overcome with regret. He'd lost his wife to a fever after only two years of marriage, when they'd lived for a brief time in the wettest and most mosquito-plagued part of Missouri. Kate had only been an infant, and Bruin had brought her West, where the air was crisp, dry, and healthful. He'd even briefly attempted to raise his daughter. It hadn't worked out, so he'd found some nice folks to raise her in a Christian manner while he tried to make something of himself in many occupations, all of them unsatisfactory and unprofitable.

His Kate had been in her teens and a stranger when he'd taken to robbing stagecoaches, and damned if the first boy she'd fallen in love with wasn't Link Cochran. "He fooled us both," Bruin told his mule. "I knew my Kate was too young to get hitched, but that damn Link swept her off of her feet."

So great was Bruin's anguish for the loss of his wife and child that tears ran freely down his bearded cheeks. He had been the one who had allowed Kate to wed Link, and he'd been the one who first showed his wild and handsome son-in-law how easy it was to rob a stagecoach. But what he hadn't taught Link was how to kill without a conscience. Kate hadn't believed her husband had been responsible for the killings, and so she'd blamed her father.

"Maggot, how on earth could I defend myself against the man she loved and who had fooled us both? And by then she was carrying her own child, Ophelia. A girl I ain't seen but maybe three times in my life, and then only at a distance."

By this time Bruin was crying so hard, he had to rein Maggot off the road and turn his face to the mountains. Several wagons passed, and their occupants stared at the huge, sobbing man on the huge white mule, but no one said a comforting word. Finally, Bruin wiped his eyes dry, then honked into his filthy handkerchief.

"Life don't ever go as you want or expect," he told Maggot. "A fella makes just a few mistakes and they'll haunt him until the day that he dies."

Bruin continued on into Prescott. He wondered if Kate and Ophelia were still living in this town. And while he wanted more than anything to visit and give them gold and whatever else they might need to make their lives easy, Bruin knew that Kate was too proud to admit that she had also made the mistake of her own life by marrying Link Cochran.

"What if I ran into him on the street or in a mercantile?" Bruin asked out loud. "What if he's changed his name and gotten respectability?"

It was not a strong likelihood, yet Bruin knew it was possible. Perhaps Kate had transformed her wild and vicious young husband into a God-fearing man.

"Naw," Bruin decided out loud. "I've known bad men that got religion and turned out good, but I never met an evil one like Link who turned over a new Leaf. And we swore to shoot each other should we ever meet again."

It was all so troubling that Bruin resolved just to do one thing at a time in Prescott and see how the cards fell. First, he'd find a couple of good men to help him, and then he'd locate the mining office and file his claim. After he mined out the gold in the Superstitions, he'd return to Prescott and see if he could make amends with his daughter and actually come to know little Ophelia.

"I wonder if she still has red hair like her mother," Bruin said out loud. "It was a pretty color . . . not real bright red, but more the color of autumn leaves or dried blood."

Bruin just didn't know if his daughter would ever speak to him again, much less accept the truth about her husband being a cold-blooded killer. Didn't know if she was still married to Link Cochran, or if she still loved him, or if Ophelia had grown up good . . . or bad. She might be like her mother, but she also might have become twisted like her father. Women, he reckoned, could go just as bad as men, though it happened less frequently.

"My granddaughter would be . . . Maggot, she'd be about

thirteen. Isn't that amazing! Probably tall like me and her mother too. Bet she's real pretty."

Bruin rode into the Prescott Valley with a dead certain conviction that, no matter what happened, he would never hurt Kate or Ophelia.

"If that means never again speaking of what happened that day those people on the stagecoach were gunned down, then so be it," he vowed. "I had my chances and I made my mistake. I should have killed Link that very day, but I didn't. Now, I got to sleep with the ghosts that haunt me, and I most likely will do so to my dying day."

Bruin tried to think of the good things in his life in order to improve his sad frame of mind. There weren't a lot of good things to recollect because his own childhood had been marred by feuding parents and a drunken and abusive father he'd always hated. But he had loved his young wife, and during their brief time together, there were many bittersweet memories. And with the discovery of gold, he still had a future . . . if that damned Link didn't kill him or he wasn't recognized in Prescott and sent to the Yuma Prison.

"Maggot," he proclaimed, "I would not mind living in this valley. With our gold, we could buy a little ranch and maybe find some happiness. The world is changing fast. I was born in Pennsylvania in the year 1827, and that was long before the gold rushes, the Civil War, the telegraph, and the railroads coming West. I am told that John Quincy Adams was our President that year, but he was not popular. I wonder who is President of the country now."

In response, the ornery mule twitched its great ears and continued along the road. Since there was growing traffic, he was now able to flash his teeth at other horses and mules and enjoy their fear.

Bruin removed his hat and let the sun warm his head, face, and beard. He would have liked to have removed his leather shirt, which was hot and was not very clean, but thought that would be showing a lack of manners. When passing others, he was careful to make sure that Maggot's teeth were out of range of other animals, but there was nothing he could do about his poor impression, and few horsemen or drivers even gave him a howdy or a smile.

He had always thought Prescott's five-thousand-foot altitude to be ideal. The town was located in a large valley ringed by immense ponderosa pine forests and fed by the cool waters of Granite Creek. Bruin knew that it had been a favorite place to winter for the early fur trappers, and later had been visited by Forty-Niners, who had stayed only for a short time before rushing on the storied California gold fields and later the famous Comstock Lode in Nevada.

Prescott Valley had become permanently established by whites in 1863, when Camp Whipple was created and staffed by two companies of California Volunteers. Fearful of a Confederate takeover, President Abraham Lincoln and Congress had declared Arizona to be a territory. A fine log capitol building was constructed in the center of the new town, and Prescott began to flourish. For a brief time, and for political reasons, the territorial capital had been moved to Old Tucson, but now it was back in Prescott and the town was prospering not only because of Fort Whipple, but also because of cattle ranching, mining, and logging.

"Maggot," he said as they rode up Gurley Street with its busy hotels, saloons, and businesses, "the first thing we'll do is find a livery where I'll have 'em feed you their best hay and oats. After that, I'll find a good hotel and then the mining office where I'll file our claim. If all goes well, I'll hire a couple of halfway honest and capable men, outfit ourselves, and we'll be heading back to the Superstitions.

As he passed a noisy saloon called the Bottom Dollar, Bruin couldn't help but smile as he saw a drunk being tossed out the door by a rather large woman with a dress that didn't hide much of her bosom. The drunk landed in the street, somersaulted, then jumped right up and charged back through the saloon's batwing doors. Before Bruin had passed, out he came again, and this time the big woman was assisted by a fancy gambler wearing a sparkling diamond on his little finger.

"Howdy!" Bruin called to all three.

The drunk had landed on his head and been knocked unconscious; but the saloon gal and gambler acted startled by the greeting. They didn't smile or wave, but instead went back inside.

"Not very friendly," Bruin observed. "But then, I never did cotton much to saloon people. Liquor is the devil's temptation, and I have been tempted too many times. Rye whiskey has cost me plenty, and is partly to blame for the blood I have spilled. But I have learned to drink in moderation, mostly."

The mule wasn't listening. It was an opportunist, and chose that moment to sink its teeth into the rump of a roan mare. The bite was vicious, and the mare, in its panic, charged forward to escape and busted the hitching rail.

"Behave your damn self!" Bruin hissed, slapping Maggot across the ears with his heavy leather reins. "Behave or I'll sell you to the Apache first chance I get, and then your miserable carcass will end over a roasting fire!"

Maggot was not intimidated, and kept marching along Gurley Street causing every animal in reach to cringe.

Bruin found a livery, and made sure his mule was kept away from all other animals explaining, "He's better off being in his own pen."

"He must be a mean one," the liveryman said, looking worried.

"They don't come any meaner," Bruin proudly agreed. "But he'll never quit on me and he's strong. Nothin' I hate more than weakness, be it in an animal or a human being."

The liveryman, short and balding with a potbelly as big as a lard bucket, took a tiny gold nugget that Bruin offered in payment. He bit it to make sure it was soft, and then asked, "Can I get into that white mule's corral to clean it once a day?"

"Best let Maggot in his shit," Bruin said without deliberation. "Won't hurt him none and it would be healthier for yourself."

"All right then." The man stared at Maggot. "I have never

witnessed such a huge or ugly animal. Bet he could pull an ore wagon all by his lonesome."

"Most likely, but he has his work cut out just carrying me and my outfit."

"Bet you could still heft some weight yourself, mister."

Bruin had been taught from an early age never to brag or show off, so he said nothing as he waved good-bye to his mule, collected his rifles and necessaries, and then left the livery in search of a decent hotel.

THAT NIGHT HE decided that it would be smart to wait until the day he was ready to leave Prescott before he filed his claim. That way, anyone who might be of a mind to steal it from him would have less time to act. Having made that decision, he realized the thing to do first was to find a couple of good men to hire. They didn't need to be experienced miners, but they had to be honest, able to keep their mouths shut, and good with guns.

I'll pay them two dollars a day and keep them well fed. But what will I tell them they are to do for such high wages?

Bruin chewed on that question all night, tossing and turning on his much-too-small bed, and finally getting down on the floor with his own bedroll. It was just before dawn when he came up with a solution.

I'll tell them they are needed to help me look for a place to ranch up behind the Superstition Mountains and to watch out for Apache who might want to lift our scalps.

It seemed like a reasonable explanation and one that would get him a couple of men with some ability and backbone. When they reached his claim, he could explain the true nature of his business, and then watch them constantly so they didn't try to kill him and steal his gold. It wasn't a good plan, but it was the best that Bruin could come up with, so he gave the matter no more thought.

He took a bath in the morning, but shunned a barber. Why

waste a dollar for a haircut and shave when he was going back out in a day or two?

Breakfast was steak, flapjacks drenched in maple syrup, eggs, and coffee. It wasn't enough, so he had a second breakfast, and then he went looking for a couple of good men.

Instead, he saw Kate and Ophelia. Bruin froze in his tracks and stared. Other people on the crowded boardwalk had to angle around him into the street because he took up so much space.

Bruin Henry did not notice anyone but his red-haired daughter and granddaughter. He did not know what to do except gape at the two women. Kate had changed dramatically, and not for the better. She looked old, although she was still young. Her hair was still a beautiful russet red, but it had streaks of gray, and Bruin saw that she was painfully thin and walked with the aid of a cane.

A cane!

A powerful and involuntary sob escaped Bruin's lips, and he took a halting step forward, but tripped over something and fell hard. Everything seemed to freeze in that moment of time. Bruin's eyes had never diverted from the pair, and now they saw him.

"Bruin?" Kate breathed. "Father!"

He scrambled to his feet, not sure if he should run to them . . . or away from them. "Kate. Ophelia."

It was all he could say.

And then they stepped forward, Kate looking old and sick and weak, Ophelia looking confused and angry.

Bruin shrank back against a wall.

"Did you come to see us," Kate asked, biting her lip and fighting her tears, "because you learned that I was dying of a cancer?"

Her words and appearance left no doubt now that his Kate *was* dying. Bruin tried to speak, but failed. It seemed as if every dream he had ever dreamed was now ashes. And when he looked down at Ophelia, all he saw was pain and burning hatred.

FIVE

—·—

"IS THAT *HIM*?" Ophelia cried. "It can't be . . . Grandpa!"

"It is," Kate said quietly. Then, looking at her father, she stepped up to Bruin and asked in a low whisper, "Father, what on earth are you doing in Prescott?"

"I came to . . ." Bruin looked around and then motioned for them to follow him off a ways where they could not be overheard. "Kate, I came to see you and Ophelia."

It wasn't the whole truth, but it was close enough because he just hadn't dared to think he might be able to speak to Kate . . . not without the gold.

"That was a mistake."

When she started to turn away, she faltered, and Bruin instinctively reached out and caught her arm. "We've got to talk!"

"I have nothing to say to you."

Ophelia pushed between them. As he'd expected, she was tall for her age, with pretty red hair and a generous smattering of freckles . . . she was the spitting image of her mother at the same age, only she was angry.

"Leave my mother alone!"

Bruin swallowed hard. "I'm not like you think," he stammered. "There are things I have to say to the both of you."

But Kate shook her head. "Go back where you came from before someone here recognizes you as an old murderer."

"I didn't kill those people! Link killed them all but one!"

"Father, you're lying!" Kate cried, grabbing her daughter and hurrying away.

"Wait!"

But they kept moving. Bruin hurried after them and when someone tried to stop him, he knocked the man down and kept going until he caught up with his daughter, who was struggling up the boardwalk.

Ophelia whirled and punched Bruin's leg wound, causing him to bellow with pain. The wound had been scabbed over and was healing, but her fist opened it up again and he felt warm blood.

"Kate," he pleaded, pushing the girl aside and blurting out his news without caring who overheard. "Kate, I came to file a claim for a gold mine I found up in the Superstition Mountains. I'm going to be rich and I want to give you and Ophelia everything. I want . . ."

"What *you* want," Kate said, turning to face him again, "has always been the issue."

She was a gentle woman, not inclined to anger, and so the presence of it caused Bruin to start. "I'm not all to blame for things," he said, knowing his words sounded weak and ineffectual. "But even if I were, you need to let me help you get healed. For yourself . . . and for Ophelia."

"Go away!"

But he wasn't listening. "We'll go back East. Get the best doctors to treat you. We'll get you healed, Kate."

"No," she said, her voice dropping. "I'm past that now. It's too late for me. It's too late even for us."

Bruin realized this was true. "What about Ophelia?"

"What do you care?"

"She's my granddaughter," he answered. "When you're gone, I've got nothing to live for except Maggot."

"Except who?" Ophelia asked, fists clenched.

"He's my white Missouri mule. We've been through a lot together. He's my only friend."

"Well I'm not your granddaughter and I hate you even more than mother does!"

"Ophelia!" Kate said, shocked.

"Well, I do!" she insisted. "Go away, you big, dirty, ugly old man!"

"Ophelia, stop that!"

In reply, the girl turned and ran up the street. Kate called after her for a moment, and then grew faint. "Bruin, please help me find a chair."

The nearest chair was occupied by a large, tough-looking man seated in front of a gunsmith's shop. Bruin didn't hesitate, but took three hobbling steps, grabbed the man by the collar, and hurled him into the street.

"Hey, are you crazy!"

"I am," Bruin said, his eyes narrowing as he picked up the chair. "And you'd best go on your way or I'll break you in half."

The man had appeared to be thinking of salving his pride by giving the older Bruin a thrashing, or worse. But after looking into the grizzled giant's flinty eyes, he lost his nerve, muttered a low obscenity, and hurried away.

"Here," Bruin said, easing his daughter into the chair. "Girl, I'll have to say that you're not looking too perky."

"I'm not feeling very perky."

She saw the blood seeping through his pants leg. "Father, what happened!"

"It's not to fret about. Just a little scratch, Kate, darlin'."

"It's a bullet wound. I can see the hole where the bullet went through your trousers. Have you just shot even more men?"

"Only a few."

Kate shook her head and swiped at tears. "You haven't changed one bit after all this time."

"Yes, I have! The men I killed were trying to steal my gold. They would have killed me had I not gotten rid of them first. It was self-defense."

"Like down in Yuma?" she said accusingly.

"No." Bruin took a deep breath. "But let's not talk about that right now. Let's get you to a doctor."

"I have a doctor here in Prescott, and there's nothing he can do to fix my cancer. It's too big. It's too late for me now."

Bruin knelt down in front of her, though it gave him considerable pain. "There must be something that can help."

"Laudanum. More and more. That's all."

"I can help," Bruin said stubbornly. "All these years I've been gone that's all I've dreamed of doing . . . helping you and Ophelia."

Kate sniffled. "Well, I'm sorry to disappoint you but I have not long left to live, and as you can plainly see, Ophelia hates you with a passion."

"Yes," he said, "and what about her father?"

"We haven't seen Link in years."

Bruin's heart swelled with hatred. "He left you and his daughter knowing you were dying?"

"No. He doesn't know." Kate looked around and saw that there were several men and women listening to them with great interest. "I guess we had better have a talk."

"That's all that I'm asking for right now. Maybe I can even talk to Ophelia."

"I wouldn't count on that . . . ever."

"Why does she hate me so?"

Instead of answering his question, Kate said, "Help me up the street. Ophelia and I rent a small room just a block away on Cortez. I need to lie down and rest."

"I'll carry you," he said, picking her up before she could protest.

THEIR ONE-ROOM LIVING space was the upstairs of a dingy little frame house. If Kate hadn't been so thin and light, it would have been a chore to climb the rickety outside stairs from the littered alley. Inside, the peaked ceiling was so low that Bruin had to bend over, and there wasn't much in the way of furniture.

"It's not bad," Bruin mumbled, trying to think of something nice, but finding that difficult as he observed the water-stained and mildewed ceiling.

"Thanks, but that's not true."

There were two beds, cots really, and an old dresser with one broken leg that had been replaced by two bricks, leaving it with a slightly tilted and scarred surface. On the dresser was a wooden cigar box filled with blue bottles and little vials, explaining why the air was permeated with a heavy and unpleasant medicinal odor. The yellow curtains were ironed, but frayed and badly faded by the relentless Arizona sun. The carpet wasn't fit for a dog to lie on, and the wallpaper was tattered.

"The landlord lives downstairs," Kate explained. "The old dear is in her eighties and sweet to us. She hasn't raised our rent in three years. When it rains or gets real cold, Mrs. Howard lets us move downstairs so we can sleep dry and warm by her fire."

Bruin opened the window, unable to stand the oppressive and once-familiar smell of medicines. "I see you got some real pretty flowers in the window box. Your mother loved flowers."

"Did she?"

Bruin was sorry he had mentioned his late wife, and immediately wanted to change the subject. "Where did Ophelia go?"

"She has friends to visit and will be back later."

"Is she going to school?"

"Yes. School is out until fall and she's a very good student. Ophelia can read and do her numbers better than I can. She's her teacher's pet, and might one day also choose the classroom."

That pleased Bruin. "That would be real fine. Katie, I always thought you'd make one hell of a good teacher."

"It's much too late now to talk about me. Besides, I want to talk about serious things."

Bruin didn't want to let loose of a pleasant thought. "Ophelia becoming a teacher is serious."

"Yes, but she'll probably change her mind. Your granddaughter also thinks it would be wonderful to drive a train." Kate managed a smile. "And yesterday, after Dr. Miller departed, Ophelia decided she wanted to become a doctor."

"A *woman* doctor?" Bruin's eyebrows lifted with surprise and just the slightest hint of disapproval. "Maybe she could be a nurse."

Kate started to reply, but then suddenly, her whole body stiffened and she moaned, causing Bruin to jump forward and crack his head on the low ceiling. "Kate, darlin', are you all right?" he shouted, dropping to his knees and noticing how she struggled for breath. Long, anxious minutes passed and her breathing slowed until, in as calm a voice as if she were asking for a bit of sugar to put in her tea, Kate said, "Please bring me my laudanum."

"Which bottle?"

"The large brown one."

She poured about two fingers in a shot glass, then drank it and coughed. "Water, please!"

There was a white porcelain pitcher on the out-of-kilter dresser. With his hands shaking so bad he spilled water, Bruin filled a glass. After Kate drank, she sighed and closed her eyes and her color improved. "I'll feel much better in a few minutes and then we'll talk."

Bruin fought back tears as he huddled at her side. He remembered waiting for his young wife to die many years earlier and how, in the last terrible days of her struggle, she had worn the same pall of death.

Damn this cruel world! Why is it that the Lord takes the good and lets the bad live? Why isn't there any earthly justice!

He blew his nose lustily in his handkerchief and stared at

the flowers, which were moving slightly in the warm breeze. He thought about how he'd used to rock Kate after her mother had died, and how he'd done nearly everything he could to support her, but town jobs were hard to find and Bruin had never been good with numbers. He'd tried to clerk in a store, but the addition and subtraction took him so long, he upset the customers and it had gotten him fired. He'd also attempted to learn the gunsmith trade, but his fingers were too thick and lacked the touch. He'd attempted to break wild mustangs, but he was too big and knew he'd never have the skill of the smaller, quicker bronc-busters.

There had been a few moneyed widows that Bruin supposed he could have married. One, Mrs. Ebberfelt, had taken a real shine to him and she had a house in town, but she also had a sharp tongue, and he'd once seen her slap her own son, a lying and worthless bully. And then there was Mrs. Connelly from Dublin, Ireland, and Lord, could she cook! But the trouble was, she'd liked to nibble all day in her kitchen and had gotten so big and fat she could hardly even waddle. She had been sweet on him, but Bruin could not have imagined mounting her in a four-poster bed strong enough to support their immense combined weight. Why, hellfire, he'd have had to go under the floor of their bed and add structural support.

There had been other women, some not so respectable, that might have panned out and allowed him to keep Kate, had Bruin been able to stand living in their houses. But he'd been too proud, and he'd hated town living and taking orders from a wife he'd have been beholden to or a boss always looking over his wide shoulders.

He'd left Kate with a good Christian couple, and he'd gone off to rob stagecoaches and people traveling on the road. Trouble was, he'd spent his money as fast as it came into his hands on liquor and women. And then, down the line, he'd met Link Cochran, and that had been the end of him ever being a real father to Kate.

"Father?"

Bruin looked up at his daughter. "You feeling some better?"

"Yes. I think we need to discuss what is to become of Ophelia."

"I'll take care of her." He didn't even need to think twice about that. He'd do whatever it took so long as he wasn't arrested and sent to prison. Why, if necessary, he'd change spittoons, sweep and mop floors.

But Kate shook her head. "Ophelia needs to see her father."

Bruin felt himself stiffen, and it was all he could do to lock his jaws together to keep the poison from spilling over his lips.

"Listen," Kate said very softly, "my daughter believes that her father is a good man."

"Well," Bruin snapped, "girls and boys also believe in fairy tales, goblins and witches, and Jolly Old St. Nicholas. But sooner or later, they have to be told the truth."

"I have told Ophelia the truth."

Bruin blinked. "What did you tell her?"

"I told her that her father has done some things that he shouldn't. I told her the same was true of you."

"But she thinks I'm a murderer!"

Kate pursed her lips and gathered her thoughts. "I told Ophelia that you and her father both have had long struggles with Satan, but always tried to do better."

He leaned forward. "You told her that?"

"Yes. I explained that we live in an imperfect world and that imperfections were a part of being human. Some people just have more than others, but we are all sinners and need forgiveness in order to gain our place in heaven."

"And what did she say to that?"

Kate turned her head and studied him carefully. "Ophelia believes that if she could see and talk to her father, she could save his soul."

Bruin couldn't believe his ears. He was momentarily stunned, then blurted out, "And what about *my* soul?"

"I'm truly sorry, but Ophelia is convinced that you are way beyond redemption."

"Why!" he cried. "Why am I beyond hope but not Link?"

"You *know* why."

Yes, he did know. "Because you told her that it was me that gunned down those passengers," he said hopelessly.

Kate reached out and touched his arm. "Father, for many years I thought that was true despite you vowing it was not. I couldn't bring myself to believe that my husband . . . Ophelia's father . . . was the real killer."

"What do you believe now?"

Her head rolled back and forth. "I simply don't know."

Bruin slammed his fist down on his knee. "Kate, you have to believe that I'm telling the truth. I only shot the one guard and—"

"Then you are *still* a murderer!"

A heavy silence fell between them and Bruin didn't know what to say because Kate was right . . . he was a murderer. He deserved to be hanged long ago. He was willing to accept his guilt, and even, at times, had thought to turn himself in to the authorities down in Yuma just to put an end to his corrosive guilt. But what ate at him almost as much had always been the way that Kate had gone on believing in the innocence of her husband.

"I'm not leaving you this time," Bruin vowed with his big fists clenched. "You can think what you want of me, but I'm not leaving until . . ."

He couldn't say it. Couldn't say that he would remain until she was gone from this world and its trials.

"Father, I want only one thing of you. Honor just my one dying request and I'll forgive you forever."

His spirit soared. "What is it?"

"I want you to take Ophelia and find her father."

"What!"

"That's what I'm asking. It's *all* that I'm asking."

His spirits plummeted and he shook his shaggy head, his

voice pleading, "Anything but that. Link might even be dead . . . if Ophelia is lucky."

"He might be dead and buried. I thought of that a great deal these past few years. But then again, he might be alive. And if he is, your granddaughter needs to see her father and make up her own mind about what kind of a man Link really is."

"Kate, you must know what he is!"

She closed her eyes and whispered, "Yes, I'm afraid that I do. But I couldn't tell Ophelia that and neither can you, because it would put a stain on her soul and darken her life with unresolved questions that would never give her any peace. And besides, she wouldn't believe either of us anyway."

Bruin didn't understand. "I can see why Ophelia would never believe me . . . but why not you?"

"You don't understand the mind of a girl," she said. "They need to believe in their father's basic goodness and they need . . . heroes."

"Heroes?" He actually scoffed at the notion. "There are no heroes . . . or at least I've never met any. Good, honest, and brave folks? Sure! But heroes . . . Kate, you just told me that all humans have faults. Why wouldn't Ophelia believe that about her father?"

"Because she never really had a complete father, only pieces of one that she filled out in her mind. Link was rarely around us and when he did show up, it was with gifts and hugs and laughter. You know how handsome and charming Link could be. And he stayed just long enough to remain that way in his daughter's eyes. The last time Ophelia saw her father, he bought her everything she wanted. Dresses, dolls, toys, and illusions."

Bruin was finally beginning to understand. "And so that's what is locked in her mind. This wonderful, giving father?"

"Exactly."

"And how did Link explain always leaving?"

"He told her he didn't like to be away but that he was a lawman."

"A lawman!"

The idea of Link Cochran being on the right side of the law was so outrageous that it was all Bruin could do not to bark with cold laughter. "Link is a killer!"

"He's a bounty hunter," Kate corrected. "And I'm sure that he's changed his name and built a whole new identity. I wouldn't be surprised if he even has another wife and some children tucked away."

"While he leaves you and Ophelia living like this?" Bruin demanded, throwing his hands about and feeling as if he was being strangled.

"Find him and show Ophelia the truth."

"You know we have sworn to kill each other."

"No!" Kate's voice took on more power than he'd have thought possible given her condition. "Father, if you ever hope to be anything to Ophelia, you can't kill her father."

"Even if he tries to kill me?"

"*Especially* if he tries to kill you."

Bruin shook his head. "What are you trying to do? Get me killed?"

"No," Kate whispered. "I'm trying to save Ophelia and maybe even yourself."

"But how . . ."

"Father, I only know that, if you want to redeem yourself in the eyes of God and your granddaughter, you have to show her the truth. You have to show her by deed and behavior what you are . . . and what her father is . . . and you can't do that by spilling even more blood."

His mind was spinning almost out of control. Bruin grabbed his head in his hands and rocked back and forth in anguish and confusion. "I just don't know how I could ever do what you're asking, Kate."

"Then don't! Go mine your gold and forget about me and Ophelia. Be rich and be happy."

He groaned. "I could never be happy leaving you this way and leaving Ophelia without family."

"Ophelia will be taken care of by the schoolteacher. I've

already spoken to her about that and I am sure your grand-daughter would be fine."

"Then that's what should happen."

"Is it?" Kate whispered. "Because, while Ophelia will survive and probably even succeed in life if you leave her to the care of others like you left me all those many years ago, I now believe you will go crazy and then go straightaway to hell."

"All right," he said. "But I don't think she will go with me in search of her father."

Kate managed to lift her head from her pillow. "Ophelia will if it is my deathbed wish to her."

"Then ask it," Bruin heard himself say. "Because I don't want to go on living this way and I do need redemption."

Her hand shot out and grabbed his own. "Save your grand-daughter! Father, I have prayed and it is your *only* hope."

Bruin Henry found himself nodding because he knew it was true.

SIX

—⁂—

THE DOCTOR SAID to Bruin and Ophelia, "I'm afraid that Mrs. Cochran won't last through the night."

"Doc," Bruin said, "that would be a blessing. She's suffered long enough."

Ophelia glared at him. "Not that you ever did anything to make my mother's life easier. She never had a mother or a father."

"Her mother would have loved her and so do I," Bruin said.

"If you do, you've always had a funny way of showing it."

"I can see where you'd think that."

Ophelia started to say something, and Bruin supposed that it wouldn't have been pleasant, but the doctor said, "Ophelia, your mother wants to see you in private. Try not to upset her or tax her strength."

Ophelia hurried to her mother's side and bent low with her ear to the dying woman's lips.

The doctor took Bruin by the arm. "There's nothing more

we can do. Why don't we go downstairs and give them a little time alone together."

"I'd rather stay right here, Doc."

"All right." He closed up his medical bag. "It's a tragedy
to lose one so young and good. That was one of the finest
women I've ever known, and she didn't have it easy. Thank
heavens that Ophelia has been her constant joy."

"Yeah," Bruin said. "I can see that. Does my daughter need
any more laudanum?"

"No, Mrs. Cochran is almost gone."

Bruin felt his throat constrict, and he had to bite the back
of his hand to keep from sobbing like a baby.

"If it's any consolation," the doctor said quietly, "you can
rest assured that your daughter forgave you when I first diag-
nosed the cancer and informed her that she had less than a
year to live."

"And you're sure that there was nothing that could have
been done by some big-city doctor?"

"I'm sure there wasn't. And besides, as you can see, that
simply wasn't an option given her finances."

Bruin took a deep breath. "If the timing would have been
just a little different. If Kate was just now getting sick, I
would have taken her anyplace she could have been helped.
But . . ."

He couldn't finish.

"Don't blame yourself," the doctor consoled as he was
leaving. "Life isn't fair and the good do die young."

"I know that," he managed to say.

"Then you also know that it's not how long we have on this
earth, it's what we do with the time we have."

Bruin managed to nod his head, and then the doctor was
gone.

HE HAD BEEN sitting on the floor with his head bowed in
prayer for perhaps two hours, or maybe it was far longer.

Suddenly, he heard Ophelia burst into tears and scream, "Mother, no!"

Bruin crawled over to be closer to them, but Ophelia whirled and slapped him in the face. "Don't touch her!" she shrieked. "You aren't worthy of touching my mother!"

Bruin was so shocked by Ophelia's blow and hatred that he was unable to speak.

Ophelia began sobbing uncontrollably and hugging Kate's neck. Bruin didn't know what to do or say. He'd certainly been aware that Ophelia had an intense dislike for him, but he'd not guessed the dark depth of her hatred. What was he to do about Kate's deathbed promise?

"I'll be coming back later to see her," he said as he stood up and went to the door. "Your mother forgave me and asked me to help you find your father. I mean to do that."

"Go away and never come back!"

"I *am* coming back," he vowed in a low but firm voice. "I'm going to go to the undertaker and order your mother the finest casket and burial this town has ever seen. And a big marble headstone carved with comforting words. I'll pay for everything, and I believe you will be glad for that at least."

Shoulders bent with sorrow, Bruin trudged down the creaky stairs and headed straight for his hotel room. He'd pried a floorboard up and hidden what gold nuggets he had not wanted to tote around Prescott. With his nuggets in a leather pouch, he found the town undertaker, a portly, middle-aged fellow who wore his piety for everyone to see and admire. He was a constant hand-wringer named Mr. Oswald, and Bruin let the man pick out his finest and most expensive casket, flowers, and headstone.

"I'll want the headstone placed over her grave right away," Bruin told Oswald. "Not next month or even next week."

"Very good." Oswald replied with great solemnity. "I will have my stone cutter begin the work as soon as you choose the words."

"I understand, but you can hire a stone cutter to put on Kate's full name along with the dates of her birth and death now."

"Of course!" He wrung his hands extra hard and vowed, "Mrs. Cochran will enjoy a funeral second to none. She was a wonderful lady, and you have my most heartfelt condolences."

Bruin didn't see how Kate could enjoy her funeral, and was annoyed. "Your *what*?"

"Condolences. You know, my utmost and sincere sorrow. And isn't it a comfort to know that she is already happily in heaven?"

"I hope she is," Bruin replied, feeling the bitterness on his tongue draining into his throat, "'cause her life was pretty much hell on earth."

"Oh," the undertaker said smoothly, "I really must disagree. Mrs. Cochran was always smiling and had many friends."

"If that's the case, why didn't they help her find a better place to live!" Bruin thundered in the man's pasty-white face. "She and Ophelia were poorer than church mice! Didn't anyone see the patches in their clothes? Or their shoes that were worn out, or . . .

"Oh, never mind," Bruin said, knowing that he was nearing the point of both rage and despair. "Just do what you promised or I'll wring your fat neck like I would that of a goose."

The undertaker's eyes widened and his pudgy fingers fluttered to his lips. "My good man!" he protested with shock in his voice, "I know that you are grieving, but that is no excuse to become abusive and threatening."

"I guess not," he said, ashamed of himself. "At least, not to you. Maybe I'll go find someone in a saloon that feels like fighting this old man."

"I don't doubt that you will. But what will that accomplish?"

"It'll make me feel bad someplace besides my heart."

BRUIN WAS NO fool, and knew that he was in a dangerous mood, so before he'd gone to a saloon, he'd paid for everything in gold and up front. He'd taken care of Maggot's livery bill for as long as necessary, his hotel room, and the funeral. Now, as he counted out the last of his gold on the long and gleaming mahogany bar top, he figured he had enough money left to get drunk, attend the funeral, and then outfit himself and two men. After he returned from the Superstition Mountains with his fortune, he'd look up Ophelia and see if she still felt the same way about hating him.

No doubt Ophelia would still refuse to go along to find Link. Then, by damn, Bruin would do it himself. There was no choice because he'd promised Kate on her deathbed. He'd scour the whole country, if necessary, to find Link Cochran and bring him back to Prescott alive. Beat to hell maybe, but alive. And then, he'd make Link admit that he'd been the one to kill all but one of those folks on that Yuma-bound stage years ago.

"What will you have to drink, old-timer?" the bartender asked, staring at Bruin's buckskin pouch filled with gold. "You can afford the best the house has to offer."

Bruin glanced around the rough little saloon whose name was crudely painted on a sign outside, but had already been forgotten. "Hell," he snarled, "I ought to be able to buy this damn rat's den with the money in my pouch."

The bartender's smile turned rancid. "Well, I doubt that. What's your damn pleasure?"

"Rye whiskey. A bottle of your best."

"Coming right up."

When the whiskey was placed before him, Brain paid the man and retired to the farthest, darkest corner of the stinking saloon. The whiskey was good and bottled in Kentucky. Bruin knew that was true because he'd drunk Kentucky whiskey in Kentucky, where folks took pride in their liquor, unlike in Arizona, where they just wanted something to bend their brains.

He drank fast for the first hour, back turned to the room and uncaring that he was the center of attention among the dozen or so other rough customers, and certainly the main topic of their conversation. Then he got up and moved over to the bar, again knowing he was a little drunk, but not so much that he didn't know exactly what he would do next.

"What do you want?" the bartender demanded. "I can see you still have some left in that bottle."

"A quality cigar."

"Cost you four bits."

"That'll be fine."

The bartender opened a glass case, and fished around until he had a large cigar in his hand. He slammed it down on the bar. "You're a demanding old bastard and I don't like your tone of voice."

"You don't?"

"No. And you need to buy a clean shirt."

Bruin heard the snickers, and then the bartender snarled, "That'll be two bits."

Bruin picked up the cigar and asked for a match.

"Pay for it before you light it!" the bartender demanded.

"I never pay until I've had a taste," Bruin said, eyeing the cigar skeptically. "For all I know, this might be a common dog turd."

He put it to the nose test, and it smelled awful. "Yep," he proclaimed, "I think it *is* a dog turd."

"Mister," the bartender said, his expression growing ugly, "you had better do as you're told in my saloon. Otherwise, you're getting roughed up and then thrown out the door."

"You gonna do that by your lonesome?"

"Me and my regular customers, who also happen to be my friends. There's plenty enough here to do the job." He raised his voice. "Ain't that right, boys!"

Bruin heard the chorus of agreement. He turned to the nearest man. "Say, friend, have you got a match?"

The man sneered, "Yeah, but I'm sure as hell not giving it to you."

"Damn unfriendly place I'm in," Bruin mused aloud as he broke the cigar in half. "Damn unfriendly."

The bartender stared at the broken cigar and his voice filled with anger. "Why you dirty old—"

He didn't get to finish because Bruin shoved the stub of the cigar halfway down his throat, grabbed his hair, and slammed his jaw down on the bar's top.

"Boys," Bruin shouted, "your friend is choking and needs a drink. I'll give him some of my good Kentucky whiskey and maybe that will clear his throat and improve his manners!"

The men around him were so surprised that Bruin actually had time to grab his unfinished bottle, twist the bartender's head back, and pour whiskey down his clogged gullet. It was a good thing he did so, because the bartender was turning purple.

"There," Bruin said, slipping his gold pouch under his belt for safekeeping as he studied men with fight written all over their faces. Suddenly, he was feeling better than he had since arriving in Prescott. "Now who wants the other half of that cigar?"

He'd made them so mad that they charged in a wave and got in their own foolish way. Bruin leveled the first one with a straight right to the mouth, and he kicked the second attacker in the crotch, stopping him in his tracks and making him howl. Then Bruin ducked a roundhouse punch and drove a vicious uppercut that lifted the third man completely off his feet. Bruin hit him again before he touched the ground, and put him out of the fight permanently.

The next one drew a knife, and Bruin felt a burning sensation as cold steel sliced across his shoulder. He grabbed the man by the hair and hurled him over the top of the bar into a counter of bottles and glasses. They shattered, and Bruin's knees buckled slightly as a fist stuck him in the side of the head. He took another punch, and drove his shoulder into someone bulling him toward the door. They shot out into the sunlight and crashed over a hitching rail into the street.

Bruin grabbed the man by the throat and shook his head like a terrier would a sewer rat before hammering him with both of his fists. He was so consumed by rage that he screamed down at the semiconscious man, "You want more from this dirty old man!"

"No, please!"

Bruin climbed off his chest and staggered over to the nearest horse trough. He saw Ophelia staring at him from across the street a moment before he waved and ducked his head under the water. It was cool, and he held it there for a long, delicious minute before coming up for air.

That turned out to be a mistake because the next thing Bruin knew, his head was split in half and he was pitching back into the horse trough without thought or feeling.

OPHELIA SAW THE big marshal come up behind her grandfather. Marshal Kilpatrick was a hard and dangerous man, and so she wasn't surprised when she saw the fury on his face. Kilpatrick drew his gun, only instead of sticking it into Bruin's back and arresting him, he reversed his grip and used it as a club. Ophelia swore she could hear the crack of bone as the handle of the marshal's Colt revolver struck the back of Bruin's skull. And when her grandfather pitched over into the horse trough, her eyes widened and she took a few involuntary steps forward, then froze in the street.

"Who is this man?" the marshal shouted at no one in particular. "Anyone know who he is?"

Ophelia almost answered, but bit her lip and held her silence.

Meanwhile, her grandfather was still head-down in the horse trough.

Moments passed as the marshal shouted at everyone who was on the street. Someone must know him.

A man with a bloodied face and wearing a white apron staggered out into the street cursing. "Arrest that man, Marshal. He's wrecked my saloon and beat up a half dozen of my best customers. I demand he be arrested!"

Ophelia hardly heard what the bartender was saying as she moved across the street knowing that her mother's father was drowning but no one was trying to save his life.

Then, suddenly and mostly against all reason and her own

will, Ophelia raced past the marshal, grabbed Bruin's long, shaggy hair, and hauled his head out of the water trough.

"Ophelia," the marshal said, spinning around and holstering his gun. "Do you know him?"

"Sure! He's my . . . my mother's old uncle."

It was a lie and badly told, but it worked because Kate had told her that she could never reveal who grandpa was or he'd probably be hanged. And while she hated Bruin Henry, she didn't want his hanging to be her doing.

"Well, he's going to jail," Kilpatrick said. "And he'd better have some money to pay the saloon damages."

The bartender ran up and cried, "He's got a pouch filled with gold, Marshal. It's under his damn belt."

The bartender would have snatched it up if Ophelia hadn't jumped first and gotten the pouch herself. Rising up, she cried, "This is my uncle's gold and he's using it for my mother's funeral! None of you are stealing it!"

Marshal Kilpatrick glared at her. "Give the pouch to me, Ophelia. I'll keep it safe."

But she knew better. Everyone in Prescott knew that the marshal padded his pockets with whatever pickings he could get from those he arrested. Usually, it wasn't much, but her grandfather was such a brute and fool that he was carrying plenty of gold.

"It's for my mother's funeral!"

"Ophelia, give me that pouch!"

"No!"

Marshal Kilpatrick's cheeks reddened even more when several bystanders shouted out to leave the girl and her gold alone. But even with that, Ophelia saw how his eyes filled with greediness. When Kilpatrick lunged at her with his arms open wide, Ophelia was quick enough to elude his grasp. She lit out up the street dodging between wagons and horses until she left the infuriated lawman far behind.

SEVEN

—ᴡᴡ—

"MARSHAL KILPATRICK IS *not* getting this gold," Ophelia shouted, ducking under a fence and then flying across a cow pasture.

She didn't stop running until she reached a stand of tall cottonwoods where she had often played in her younger days. Ophelia found a good hiding place under a fallen tree and quickly buried most of the nuggets, realizing that she couldn't hide from Marshal Kilpatrick forever. Sooner rather than later, he'd find her and want Bruin's gold and she'd suffer the consequences.

He wouldn't dare to kill me, but the marshal would take a whip to my backside even if he had to do it with me gagged so nobody heard me screaming in his jail cell.

Ophelia sat fidgeting for a long time, wondering why in the world she'd interfered to save Bruin Henry. She endured waves of anger at her foolishness, followed by moments of confusion and even a dose of pride. It was the first time in her life that she'd willingly put her neck in a noose. Normally, she was calm, cool, and in control. But with the death of her mother, her mind was scattered and she was acting crazy.

"Oh, darn it," she wailed up at the leaves waving in a soft breeze, "what have I done!"

Moments later, Ophelia had her answer. "I have tried to save a human being's life and become a thief of his gold."

The more she thought about it, the more Ophelia felt proud of herself. Stupid, yes, but also brave. But had she really saved that terrible old man's life? Marshal Kilpatrick was cunning and dangerous. He had struck her grandfather so hard that he might have permanently damaged old Bruin Henry's already ruined brain.

Ophelia shivered although the air was warm. It had been awful to see that horrible old man with his dirty backside stuck up in the air like a stinkbug while he lay helpless and drowning.

Old Bruin deserves to be hanged . . . not drowned. Nobody deserves to die that way, not even a vicious or rabid animal.

Ophelia was afraid to return to town until darkness began to fall on the valley. She knew that her teacher would be worried, and maybe a few others as well, but she also wanted to give Marshal Kilpatrick time to cool down. Was Bruin Henry dead . . . despite her action? If so, there was nothing that could be done about that. Ophelia had seen the bartender all battered and bleeding, and she had little doubt that her grandfather had left other drinking men in even worse condition.

He was horrible! A terrible, filthy, and murdering ogre that should have been hanged years ago for killing those stagecoach men and their passengers down in Yuma. And for putting her father on the run for crimes he could not possibly have committed.

Ophelia saw that she had torn her dress when she'd ducked under the fence. She'd been in such a panic she'd not noticed it then, but now she could see that the dress was ruined. Oh, well, she hadn't liked the dress anyway. It was frayed, faded, and a constant source of embarrassment. Other kids her age made fun of it, and she'd only worn the danged thing because of her mother's insistence.

Tears filled her eyes. The funeral would be tomorrow, and now she didn't even have this awful dress to wear. What would she do? Wear a gunny sack?

Ophelia cried, remembering her mother and how they'd always been there to help each other. Her mother had worked long hours in a laundry owned by a German couple who had not been nice. They'd held up over the years, and whenever her father had been able, he'd visited bringing her gifts and stories of the places he'd been and the things he'd seen. Why, her father had even traveled to Washington, D.C., to be honored by the President of the United States! He was a very brave lawman, and was always putting his life at risk in order to help people. United States Marshal Link Cochran was the kind of man that pretenders like Marshal Kilpatrick could never hope to be. Compared to her father, Kilpatrick was a weakling and a worm.

I will use just a little bit of this gold to buy a dress for the funeral, and then I will decide what I am to do next.

That decision made, Ophelia pushed off the log and headed back to town, keeping a close watch that the marshal didn't catch her by surprise. She knew that her friend and schoolteacher would have heard of her craziness and be frantic about her welfare. Ophelia decided that she had better go visit her right now and try to explain what she'd done and why.

But then, she'd have to make up her own mind about matters. What to do and if she could stay in Prescott, or if she should go find her father whom she had not seen in too many years.

"If he's dead like Mother, I will just kill myself," Ophelia said aloud as she trooped into Prescott wondering if Marshal Kilpatrick had killed Bruin Henry.

IT WAS DARK in the cell when Bruin awoke with a splitting headache. He groaned and rolled on the stone floor until he was sitting upright and leaning against the wall. There was a pale, flickering light across the room, but between himself and that light were the heavy iron bars of his cell undulating like heat waves on a lonely desert road. Bruin stared through them at a man sitting at a desk eating his supper from a tin plate by the light of a kerosene lamp. Bruin knew it was a tin plate because the man's spoon made a repetitive scraping sound. He was big and wore a shiny marshal's badge pinned to his vest. His boots were polished, and the gun on his hip had grips made of polished pearl or bone.

Bruin's fingers gently explored his scalp, and traced the thick ridge of scab, then flakes of dried blood on his face. He took a deep breath and scooted over to the bars, then dragged himself erect.

"Are you the one that broke my gourd?" he croaked.

The marshal didn't stop eating, and the scraping noise sounded unnaturally loud in the cramped office built of mortar and heavy river stone.

Bruin pulled himself tight against the bars and squinted at the lamplight. "Mister, are you the marshal of Prescott?"

"I ain't Robert E. Lee," the man drawled, still not bothering to glance in Bruin's direction.

Bruin tested the bars and found that they were firmly planted. He turned and saw a small, high cell window, and would also test those bars.

"I can see you looking around, but you aren't going anywhere, old man."

Bruin licked his lips and tried to gather his thoughts. Did this man know his real name and that there was a bounty on his head down in Yuma? If so, his goose was cooked. "Marshal," he said, clearing his throat and spitting on the cell floor. "I know that I roughed some fellas up in that saloon, but it was a fair fight. They gave as good as they got."

"No, they didn't. You beat the hell out of them." The marshal finally looked his way. "What kind of a man are you?"

"A foolish one."

"I understand that Mrs. Cochran was your daughter and that Ophelia is your granddaughter."

"That's right."

"Hard to believe," the marshal drawled. "What's your last name?"

"Johnson," he said, without hesitation, using an old and familiar alias. "William Johnson."

"I very much doubt that, but Ophelia will set the record straight when I catch up with her."

Bruin didn't like the sound of that, but knew he was in no position to antagonize this man who had almost killed him with a vicious pistol-whipping. "What have you arrested me for?"

"For being drunk and disorderly. You caused great damage to both human beings and property. Also, you resisted arrest."

"I didn't resist arrest!" Bruin protested. "You clubbed me from behind. Marshal, all you'd of had to do is just tell me to stop fighting and behave."

The marshal wiped his lips with the care of a cat. He had a thick red handlebar mustache. When he'd cleaned himself well, he twisted the ends using mustache wax he'd taken from his desk drawer.

As Bruin's mind cleared even more, he could see that the marshal was a large, handsome man and one fussy about his appearance. Bruin knew that vain men were often the most dangerous because they were overly sensitive about their looks and whatever impression they made. He would have to be very careful.

"Marshal, I do have some gold. You probably took it along with my knife and other personals. I am sure there is enough in my pouch to more than pay for the damages."

"I'm sure there was, Mr. Johnson."

Bruin didn't like the sound of that. "What do you mean . . . *was*?"

"I mean that your granddaughter ran off with your pouch of gold."

"Little Ophelia?"

"That's right." The marshal tweaked the tips of his mustache upward. "But I'll catch her soon enough."

"Marshal, you shouldn't scare that poor girl."

"Dammit, to me she's just a dirty orphaned thief!"

Bruin was taken aback by the outburst. Had he not been behind bars, he would have tried his best to teach this man respect for a child. But since he was behind bars, there was nothing Bruin could do but say, "Ophelia just lost her mother . . . my daughter. She's upset, but I'm sure she'll be back with my gold."

"I doubt that," the marshal fumed. "However, the funeral is tomorrow and I'm sure Ophelia will attend the ceremony. When she does, I'll have men posted to grab the little monkey. She'll either hand over that gold pouch or I'll break her arms, then her damned legs and then her neck."

Bruin was appalled. "You'd do a vile thing like that to an innocent child?"

"Ophelia is a thief and I'll do what's necessary."

"What kind of marshal are you!" Bruin shouted, causing a fork of pain to skewer his brain. "She's just a motherless little girl, for crying out loud!"

The marshal stood up and swaggered over to the cell stopping just beyond Bruin's reach. "I don't have time for your mouth, so shut it up or I'll come in there and shut you up permanently."

Bruin retreated to the window wall, then raised and clenched his big fists. "Come on in," he challenged.

Kilpatrick reached for the cell key tied to his belt, but then wisely reconsidered. "I'll deal with you later. But right now, it's time to lock up for the night." He smiled coldly. "It's a real pity that you won't be able to attend your own daughter's funeral tomorrow morning. There probably won't be many people there. The woman wasn't of importance in Prescott, and too poor to be mourned or remembered."

Bruin hadn't thought of that, and the idea of being locked up while his Kate was being laid to rest almost overwhelmed him with guilt and sorrow. "Marshal," he cried, "I'll pay you more gold than Ophelia's got."

The man hesitated at the front door. "Is that right? Tell me where the gold is and I'll set you free tonight."

"It's not here. It's . . . it's up in the Superstition Mountains."

"Then it does me no good."

"But I could take you there."

"Not interested. For all I know, you stole the gold from someone else."

"No, sir! I struck it rich."

Kilpatrick sneered. "I've heard that one before. Sorry, but you'll either cough up gold before the funeral or you're staying here until hell freezes over."

"But I need to be at that funeral! Marshal, at least let me go in handcuffs or . . ."

But Kilpatrick wasn't listening and was gone.

Bruin shook the bars, but they offered no hope of loosening. He reached up to the tiny barred window, but it was also solid and too small for him to crawl through.

I'm stuck, he thought. *I'm gonna miss my daughter's funeral and I've got no one to blame but my own miserable self.*

Bruin felt terrible, but the physical pain was nothing compared to the guilt he felt about getting drunk and being responsible for the mess he was in. Clearly, the marshal was not a reasonable or even a decent man. Anyone who would break a girl's bones for a pouch of gold was a craven coward totally lacking in conscience.

"I have to get out of here and find Ophelia," he kept repeating aloud over and over. "I got to find that girl and save her from the marshal."

Bruin paced back and forth in his dirty little cell. When he grew tired, he tested every stone in the floor seeking one that might be pried up and used to batter the bars. But there was not a one that he could rip free, and so he lay on his back with the smell of urine and sweat heavy in his nostrils, and closed his eyes trying to think of something . . . some way that he could get out of this mess.

Earlier that day he'd been dreading the thought of having to go after Link Cochran. Now, he'd give anything just to have that opportunity despite the fact that it very well might get him killed.

SOMEWHERE IN THE night he started dreaming about Maggot and the time that the big mule had gotten stuck in quicksand on the Gila River. Bruin had forced the mule onto a bottomless sandbar. Maggot had immediately bogged down and then struggled and struggled, his eyes rolling around in his head like two beans in a wooden bowl.

On the hard, filthy floor of his cell, Bruin Henry's own body jerked and twitched violently as he relived that awful time at the river. He'd bailed off the stricken mule with his rope and rifle, then lassoed Maggot and tried to drag the terrified mule free. Together, they'd fought that sucking sand, but it had irresistibly kept pulling Maggot in deeper and deeper, until only his head and neck were visible.

Bruin's closed eyes shuttered rapidly as the dream unfolded and this time, instead of a teamster coming to their rescue just minutes before Maggot would have vanished, the mule *did* vanish with its great brown eyes pleading for help and braying piteously.

"No!" Bruin screamed, thrashing and groping blindly on the dirty stone floor.

"Grandpa! Grandpa Henry, please wake up!"

Bruin was covered with cold sweat. "What . . ."

"It's Ophelia."

He wiped his face dry with his sleeve. "Ophelia?"

"We've got to talk."

Bruin shook off the nightmare and struggled to his feet. The window was too high to see through, but just the sound of that girl's voice was a blessing from above, like that of an angel. "I sure am glad to hear you, Ophelia."

"I'm not glad to be here, but the marshal shouldn't have hit you that hard. Now, he's after me and I don't know what to do. My schoolteacher is afraid for my life and yours as well."

"Then she's smart," Bruin opinioned. "The marshal said you took my gold. He said he'd break your arms, legs, and even your neck when he caught you at the funeral tomorrow."

"He said that?" she asked, voice trembling.

"Yes, he did," Bruin gravely assured her. "I believe him and you'd be wise to do the same. He's a mean man, Ophelia."

"I know!"

"So what are we to do?" Bruin asked. "Unless the marshal gets my gold, he'll hurt you and keep me locked up in here until hell freezes over."

Bruin waited, but he couldn't hear Ophelia doing anything but breathing fast, which told him she was scared near to death.

"Ophelia, I hate the idea of missing your mother's funeral, and I sure can't stomach the thought of that marshal breaking your bones."

"I'll give him the gold," Ophelia decided aloud. "I spent only a little on a new dress for mother's funeral. So I'll give him your gold and then he'll set you free and you can go away."

"I'm still going to find your father."

"I know. And I'm going along so, when you meet, you don't shoot my father in the back like you did those people down by Yuma."

Bruin decided this was not the time or place to argue with his granddaughter. If she was going with him . . . even for the wrong reasons, that was enough.

"Just remember that I'm not doing this for you," Ophelia insisted. "I'm doing it for Mother. It's what she asked me to do and it was her last wish."

"I understand. I told the marshal that my name was William Johnson. I doubt he believed me. I couldn't let him

know who I really was or he'd have sent my body to Yuma for
the reward."

"It would have served you right."

"I know that to be true. But Ophelia, when you give the
marshal my gold, do it with plenty of people around. Otherwise, he'll take the gold and maybe hurt you bad anyway."

"I will make sure that I am in the company of good people
tomorrow at the funeral," she replied. "And that the marshal
promises to set you free."

Bruin shook his head. "I wish you could do it *before* the funeral. It will cause me great pain not to see your dear mother
laid properly to rest."

Ophelia said something, but Bruin couldn't understand it,
as she hurried away.

Well, he thought feeling lower than the belly of a snake,
*you got drunk and put an even bigger burden on that poor
girl. There can't be any bigger fool in this whole wide world
than Bruin Henry.*

EIGHT

—~m—

MARSHAL KILPATRICK RETURNED to his office just before nine o'clock the next morning, and by then Bruin had a raging thirst.

"I could sure use a cup of coffee," he said as the lawman poured himself a steaming cup from a pot he'd carried in from some restaurant. "It sure smells good."

"Yeah," Kilpatrick said, sipping noisily, then blowing a mantle of steam from his cup. "It is good. Nothing like a cup of strong coffee to get a man started on his day."

Bruin gripped the bars and waited. It was obvious that Kilpatrick had no intention of pouring him a cup.

"If I can't have coffee," Bruin finally said, "at least give me a damn cup of water."

"I guess I could do that . . . after the funeral," the man said.

Bruin's throat was so dry that he could hardly swallow. "I'm not an animal, but at least I deserve to be watered like one."

Kilpatrick glanced over at him. "I guess I could get you water . . . even coffee . . . if you come up with more gold."

His big hands clenched the bars. "So that's how it is, huh?"

"Yep." Kilpatrick grinned, and Bruin had to admit the man had a fine set of teeth. So fine that Bruin had a powerful yearning to knock them down Kilpatrick's throat.

"I told you that I had a discovery up in the Superstition Mountains. I even offered to take you there."

"So you did! But you see, I'm the elected marshal of Prescott. Now how do you think the people who voted for me would take it if I just left them for a couple of weeks to see if you're telling the truth about your gold mine?"

Bruin's head hurt, but he could still think well enough to see the marshal's reasoning. "I could give you my rifle and outfit so you knew that I was telling you the truth," Bruin said. "But I'd need my mule to get to the new gold discovery."

"Naw," Kilpatrick said, screwing up his face and then grinning. "Your mule is the only thing besides the gold worth much value. How much do you figure that big Missouri mule will get me?"

"What do you mean?"

"When I sell him."

Bruin choked off a curse. "He ain't for sale!"

"Yeah, he is! Why, I'll bet that big, ugly mule will fetch me a hundred dollars."

"He's worth a whole lot more to me than that!"

"Maybe so," the marshal said, "but a man has to take what he can get."

"This ain't right!"

"Tell you what I'm going to do, old man. I'll write up a bill of sale for your mule, saddle, and rifle. Let's give 'em a value of . . . oh . . . two hundred dollars. You'll sign the bill of sale and I'll turn you loose in time for your daughter's funeral."

"You sonofabitch."

"Now, now," Kilpatrick said as he began to write up the bill of sale. "You should be careful of your tongue or it will get you in even deeper trouble than you are already."

"Whatever you're writin', I ain't signin'," Bruin vowed.

"Don't matter," the man said, scribbling away. "I'll sign your X for you."

"You can't do that!"

"I just did," Kilpatrick said happily. "But since you've been so uncooperative, I think I'll just leave you in jail for a week or two. If you sass me . . . you'll get no food or water. That will damn sure take the pepper out of your belly. Hell, you'll be mewling like a kitten by the time I take you out of that cell and rawhide you out of Prescott with nothing but the rags you're wearing."

Bruin clenched his jaw because what he had to say to the marshal wouldn't be smart.

"What's the matter?" the marshal asked. "Cat got your tongue?"

As he lay down on a flea-and-tick-infested mattress of straw, Bruin had to remind himself that there were times when it was best to keep still. Yelling at the marshal would only inflame the man's resolve to do him ever greater harm. But now Bruin could see that there was no dealing with this man. He'd have to break out of this jail and he'd have to do it while he still had his strength.

But how? he wondered.

Nothing more was said between them for nearly an hour, and then Kilpatrick finished reading his paper and waxing his mustache. He smoothed his black suit of clothes and stood before the mirror admiring himself and giving the cock of his hat brim a lot of foolish attention.

"I'm off to your daughter's funeral now," Kilpatrick said, as if he were going to a Sunday school picnic with the prettiest girl in town. "I've got my friends on the lookout for Ophelia. There's no doubt in my mind that she'll show up for the funeral."

Bruin jumped to his feet and flung himself at the bars in a rage that shook both himself and the room. "If you harm a single hair on her pretty head, I'll find a way to kill you, so help me God!"

The threat didn't faze the marshal in the least. Still grinning, he said, "She'll either give me the gold or face the consequences. Just like yourself, old man."

After the marshal was gone, Bruin shook the bars until he was exhausted. He sat down in the darkest corner of his filthy cell and cursed the marshal and then himself for being such a fool. He'd lived what? Fifty-eight years, and he was still heaping misery on himself from his mistakes. If he'd stayed sober and hadn't gone into that saloon, he'd have shaved, washed his face, hands, and arms, and even combed his beard and hair for Kate's funeral. But now, here he was in a cell at the complete mercy of an evildoer.

The sad and pathetic position he was in, Bruin thought, was enough to break even a strong man's spirit.

IT WAS ALMOST noon before Kilpatrick arrived, and that was the longest two hours of Bruin's life. He'd tried to visualize the funeral ceremony that he'd spared no expense to make fine. He thought of passages in the Bible that would be said, and of how handsome Kate's coffin would look in the morning sunlight.

He also pictured Ophelia and her beautiful red hair, but then he saw the tears that would stream down her lovely face. But most terrible to his mind was the thought of that damned marshal and his friends grabbing the girl and forcing her to give over his gold.

It was two hours of pure hell.

"Well," Kilpatrick said, "it was a mighty fine funeral. There weren't many in attendance because Kate Cochran was nothing much to speak of, but her burial was impressive. Far more impressive than was called for."

Bruin was back on his feet. "It was paid for in advance. My daughter was a far better person than yourself. Why, Marshal, you aren't even fit to touch her coffin!"

Kilpatrick's face hardened as he settled into his office chair. "That remark just cost you a cup of water and today's food."

Bruin wasn't about to give him the satisfaction of knowing how thirsty he was now and how hungry.

"Look!" Kilpatrick cried, tossing the buckskin pouch of gold in the air and catching it with his left hand. "Recognize this?"

"It's mine."

"Was yours," the marshal corrected. "Just like your rifle, pistol, saddle, and mule. Thought you'd be interested to know that I did get a hundred dollars for that big, ugly jack. Yep! I sold him already. A fella from Flagstaff bought him, and he'll be taking that mule up to the higher country tomorrow."

"If he tries to put a rope around Maggot's neck, he will get his own neck broken!"

"Oh, I doubt that," Kilpatrick said, unfazed. "This man is an experienced muleskinner. He knows he and a few of his helpers might have to beat that white Missouri mule half to death before he takes him out of his stall."

It was all that Bruin could do to ask, "What did you do to Ophelia?"

"Why, nothing!" Kilpatrick exclaimed, looking offended. "She came right up to me even before the dirt started being pitched on that fancy coffin and handed me this gold pouch. She was crying real hard, but managed to ask that you be released. It pained me greatly to tell her that, because of your bad mouth, you'd be my guest for a couple of more weeks."

He's trying to break your spirit and he's doing a damn fine job of it. Bruin told himself again and again as he lay back down on the floor and bit his lip until it bled. *Don't give this sick excuse for a man any satisfaction. If he sees he's hurting you, he'll try even harder to leave you with nothing to fight for. He wants you to beg and wallow, but you'd better not or you're damn sure finished for certain.*

But when you get out, if you get out of here, kill him slow and make him beg for your mercy.

Kilpatrick stretched and yawned. "Well," he drawled, "I reckon I'll go have a beer and some lunch. Funerals always give me a good appetite. See you later, old man!"

Bruin said nothing as the door closed. He went back to the bars and shook them all over again, closing his eyes tight and trying to sense a single weakness. Just one bar not properly set was all he needed. Because these bars were no different than the links in even the stoutest chain . . . break one . . . and he would be free to exact his terrible vengeance.

NINE

—⁓—

BRUIN HENRY'S SPIRITS had never been lower than the day that they buried his daughter. He spent hours thinking about the only woman he'd ever loved, who had died young, and how little time he'd spent with Kate during her childhood. He could have tried harder to be a father, but he'd failed and taken what had seemed like the easy road at the time, robbing stagecoaches.

What a fool he'd been and still was! Bruin knew he'd wasted his whole life, just pissed it away in the wind. The world was unforgiving, and when a person made a bad mistake early, it was almost impossible to turn his life around for the better, and he hadn't even tried that hard. He'd become a drifter and then a prospector, still seeking the quick, easy riches. As for that old wanted poster and the reward still on his mangy head, Bruin knew that he could blame Link Cochran for taking him from being a damn good stagecoach robber to being a killer, but he'd planted the seeds of his own self-destruction long before he'd met Link.

Still, when he thought of his son-in-law, Bruin reckoned

that Link had caused him more than a fair share of misery because, not only had Link ruined his life, but he'd ruined pretty Kate's as well. And now, Bruin was bound by a deathbed promise to find Link and reunite the murdering sonofabitch with Ophelia.

If I had a rope, I'd be better off just hanging myself from those window bars than letting Ophelia find out who her father really is.

And so Bruin wished for death, or at least a profound and dreamless sleep. The day grew hot and the cell was rank and airless. It caused the fleas and the ticks to become more active, and they plagued him badly, but Bruin was alone and not in the habit of complaining. Still and all, it grated him that the marshal had left him in this cell so long without food and water. Bruin could feel his tongue swelling, and his throat was so dry that it hurt to swallow. A man could deal with hunger, but thirst was a deadly demon.

He saw the sunset color of the sky through solid bars of his window, and it set Bruin to thinking about all the sunsets he'd watched these past many years with Maggot. And now, according to the marshal, he was even going to lose his only friend and companion. They were a good pair because both of them were so ornery and independent. You couldn't force Maggot to do much of anything, so Bruin had learned to talk to him as if he were a difficult human being who had to have everything carefully explained before he'd agree to a plan of action.

"But I'm that way myself," Bruin muttered aloud. "I never could take orders from anyone. In my younger days, when I was big and some women even said handsome, I thought I knew it all and . . . if someone did know more than me . . . I resented and sometimes even tried to pick a fight with them. Now I'm sitting here in this cell and my mule is being sold along with every damn thing I own, and I'm helpless as a hen among foxes."

Bruin watched the sunset die, and wondered if he would ever be free again, and if so, if he would finally be man enough to do just a couple of things right before he cashed in his chips. Things like getting his gold out of the Superstitions and using the money to help Ophelia, and then tracking down the families of the men who had died that terrible and bloody day when he and Link had robbed the Yuma stagecoach. Bruin didn't know how he'd track those families down, but he would in order to help them with his gold.

Bruin Henry closed his eyes as darkness deepened, and then clasped his hands in front of his chest, bowed his head, and prayed. "Lord, I have sinned enough for ten men. I am one of the last sonofabitches on earth that deserve a chance to try and make up for the bad things I've done. So I'm not expecting anything, but I am saying that if I do get out of here alive and become rich, I will use my wealth to do right by others . . . starting with the families of the ones I have harmed most grievously. And I don't know what will happen if I should find Link Cochran. I have a might yearning inside me to kill him. But if it's your will, I'll not complain if he drills me first. He's younger and faster and better with a gun than me, and Ophelia thinks he's a good man. So Lord, I don't know what to do about all this trouble I'm in, but I'll trust in your wisdom and I hope you show me the way, however damned hard that might be. And I ask you to watch out for my mean old mule."

Having said his prayer, Bruin felt a measure of peace in his heart. His head still hurt awful from the pistol-whipping, his bullet wounds had reopened, the fleas and ticks were almost maddening, and he was so thirsty that he could have drunk up half the muddy Colorado. Other than that, he could endure whatever came his direction.

"BRUIN!"

He'd been dozing, and thought maybe the Lord was calling him to the Promised Land when he heard his name called. But it wasn't the Lord . . . it was Ophelia.

"Yeah," he said, his voice little more than a tortured whisper.

"I gave your gold pouch to the marshal. There wasn't anything else I could do."

"I know."

"How are you faring?"

"I'm alive. Kinda thirsty, though."

"Marshal Kilpatrick treating you all right?"

"I haven't seen him since just after the funeral. I don't expect to see him again until morning."

There was a long silence. Then Ophelia said, "If I figure out some way to get you free, will you promise not to kill my father should we be lucky enough to find him?"

Bruin frowned in the fetid darkness of his miserable cell. "I already promised that to your mother on her deathbed."

"My father doesn't think much of you. He says you deserve to die in the worst way."

"No worse than he does."

"I don't believe you," Ophelia said in a tight voice. "But . . . but that doesn't matter. I need your help to find him. How would we begin?"

"I'd start out in Flagstaff, where he was last known to be, and just follow his trail."

"But what if there isn't any trail left?"

"Everyone leaves a trail. And if I could get back to my gold, we'd have the money to go however far and wide it took to find Link. If we came to a dead end on our search, we might even hire a Pinkerton detective."

"I hadn't thought of that," Ophelia said, hope creeping into her voice. "But I doubt we'd have all that much trouble."

"Why do you say that?"

"Because my father is a United States marshal and I'll bet he's pretty famous among federal lawmen. Don't you think we'd need to start by going to Washington, D.C.?"

"We might. But I'd have the gold to buy us tickets and whatever else it took."

There was a considerable pause, and then Ophelia said, "Marshal Kilpatrick just might decide to kill you."

"I think he already has made that decision."

"Then I've *got* to get you out of there. I could steal a gun and you could get the drop on him in the morning."

Bruin shook his head in the darkness. "I don't think the marshal would go for that. He's a bully, but he's also a peacock. He's the kind of a man that would rather take his chances in a shoot-out than have anyone wound his pride."

Bruin heard Ophelia sigh. "I believe you are right about that. Then what else can we do!"

The child sounded so concerned that Bruin took heart. "I think you should go get my mule and a stout rope."

"But you wouldn't fit through that window."

"If the rope were long enough, I could tie it to one of these inside bars. Maggot could pull one or two loose from the alley, and then I'd grab my rifle and a pistol and scoot out onto the street. Most likely, I'd not be seen in the dark, and then we could leave Prescott without me killing the marshal and stirring up the whole town."

"But you said Maggot was awful and would not allow anyone to touch him."

"Yes, I did. But he is as ornery as he is smart."

Bruin remove his dirty shirt and then his pants so that all he was wearing was his red woolen long underwear. He balled his shirt and pants up and then shoved them through the high window bars. "Put 'em on when you get to the livery."

"They're way too big, and besides, these filthy old clothes won't fool a smart mule into thinking that I am you!"

"Of course not, but Maggot knows I wouldn't hand over my clothes except to someone I liked and trusted. Just talk nice to him and explain what we need to do, and then lead him up the back alleys to this window. And don't forget to put my saddle on him and bring a long, stout rope."

"You sure are asking a lot from me," Ophelia said. "I could get caught by the man who owns the livery, and then I'd be turned over to the marshal and he'd have both of us in that cell."

"Life is nothing except making hard choices. You can try bringing me the mule and a rope . . . or you can walk away and let me die at the hands of your marshal."

"All right," Ophelia finally answered. "I'll . . . ugggh!"

"What!" Bruin called.

"Your clothes stink so bad!"

"This whole mess I'm in stinks. When you get to the mule, drape my clothes over yourself, and just remember to explain everything to Maggot like he's your best friend. If he agrees, he'll let you saddle and bridle him."

"And if he don't?"

"He'll probably bite your head off," Bruin said matter-of-factly. "And then I'd feel even worse than I do right now."

Bruin didn't hear anything more from Ophelia. He dozed off and when he awoke, he gazed up at the starry heavens and figured it was well past midnight.

"I got Maggot and a rope!"

Bruin jumped up and reached his hand out of the high window. "Hand me over the rope."

"Well, aren't you the demanding one! I risk getting my head bit off by this ugly mule, then maybe killed for trying to help, and I don't even get a 'Thank you, Miss Ophelia Cochran.' My father always said you were one of the most ungrateful men he'd ever had the misfortune to meet."

"Well, I won't tell you what I thought and still think of your father," Bruin growled. "Ophelia, just hand me one end of the rope and tie the other to my saddle horn."

"I couldn't get your saddle."

"Then whose saddle did you steal?"

"I didn't get *any* saddle. They were all locked up tight in a room, so I just found a lead rope for Maggot."

Bruin resisted the impulse to swear, then demanded, "How's my mule supposed to jerk a bar or two loose without a saddle horn!"

"I'll tie the long rope around his neck."

"Ophelia, he's way too damn smart to hang himself!"

"Well," she said, sounding exasperated, "then I guess you'll just have to help him pull those inside cell bars loose, or else I'll turn him free and go home to bed. I've had a terrible day and I'm not in the mood to argue. They buried my mother today. Remember?"

He heard her sob, and felt ashamed of himself. "Of course I remember. Sorry to be so grumpy, but I don't feel right, and it hasn't been all that great a day for me either."

"Let's just try and stop arguing and get you out of there."

"Good idea."

Bruin pulled the rope inside and walked it across his cell. He'd already decided on the bar he'd start with, which seemed the most likely to pull free of its footing. He tied the rope to that bar, then set his feet on the stone and hissed, "Ophelia. Maggot, let's give it a go!"

The rope snapped taut, and Bruin threw his great strength and weight into an all-out effort. He couldn't see Maggot, but he could feel the fibers of the rope tingle and whine under an immense amount of strain. Then, just as if the Lord were helping, the bar tore free sending Bruin reeling backward into the wall. He struck it so hard that the air was knocked from his lungs and he sagged to the floor gasping like a beached fish.

"What happened?"

It took Bruin a full minute to get his lungs working again and croak, "We did it. One more bar and I can squeeze into the marshal's office."

"If you weren't so big you could probably do it right now," Ophelia complained.

Bruin didn't dignify that comment with a response, but instead called, "Give me slack."

"The mule is choking."

"What!"

"He's choking!" Ophelia cried as Bruin heard the animal's strangled breathing.

"Cut the rope!"

"I haven't got a knife!"

Bruin panicked. Without thought, he slammed into the gap where the bar had been removed and used his arms, back, and legs to bend a larger opening, then squeezed through crashing to the office floor.

The room was pitch black, but he knew where everything was located. He remembered there was a butcher knife beside the coffeepot because he'd seen Kilpatrick use it to slice a piece of beef jerky. He also knew where his gun belt and rifle were resting, and so he grabbed all of them and opened the front door.

The hour was late, but he was still lucky that nobody was passing by the marshal's office when he burst out onto the sidewalk and then ran along a dark and narrow corridor between two buildings leading back to the alley.

"Maggot," he cried, throwing himself to the ground beside the choking mule. "Maggot!"

The mule thrashed mightily at the sound of Bruin's voice, and when the knife blade finally sawed the heavy strands of rope apart, Maggot made a sound in his throat like when he'd popped out of the quicksand on the Gila river.

"He's gonna make it," Bruin breathed, stroking the mule's neck and then behind his ears.

Maggot's teeth locked on Bruin's forearm. It hurt, but Bruin knew it could have hurt far worse had the white Missouri mule been serious in wanting to do him great physical damage.

"He's gonna be fine," Bruin said, pulling Maggot to his feet. "We'll walk him up this alley to the edge of town, and then I'll go back and steal a horse for you and a saddle for me to use."

"Steal a horse!" Ophelia was shocked.

"A man has to do what a man has to do," Bruin patiently explained. "Give me my clothes. I can't be seen sneaking around here in my red underwear."

"But you can be seen stealing a man's horse and an extra saddle!"

"It doesn't matter," Bruin reasoned as he started leading a

still-gasping Maggot down the alley. "Either way, if I'm caught by Marshal Kilpatrick, I'm a dead man."

"Nobody has ever broken out of that cell," Ophelia said. "Marshal Kilpatrick is going to take that very personal. He'll get a posse and they'll come after us."

"By then we'll be fifty miles away," Bruin said. "I am a man who knows how to cover his tracks well."

She fell in beside him. "I'm sure you do, Bruin Henry. After all, you're wanted for murder."

"That's right," he replied in a voice so dry it sounded like old tree limbs cracking. "And if Kilpatrick comes after me and gets close, I'll murder him in less than a minute."

"I won't be a part of that," Ophelia vowed, and stopped walking.

Bruin stopped as well. He dropped the lead rope in his fist and said, "Girl, you have a big decision to make right now and you'd better understand the facts, which are that, come morning, your tracks will be found behind the jail and at the livery. Kilpatrick will know that you are the only one that would steal my mule and help me break out of his stinking jail cell. Do you think that he'll take kindly to that?"

She swallowed hard in the faint moonlight. "No, I guess he won't."

"And what do you think he will do to you?"

"It wouldn't be nice."

"It would be . . ." Bruin considered his next words with care. "It would be an outrage and I wouldn't be able to stop him."

"So you're saying that I'm over a barrel and really have no choice."

"When you helped me you made your choice, and now you have to just make the best of it. Like it or not, now we're both criminals in the eyes of the law."

Ophelia bent over and shook her head. "I never thought I'd come to this sorry state of affairs."

"Well," Bruin said, trying to sound sympathetic, "sometimes a person just gets in over their heads before they know it. I'm sorry about that, but I had to tell you the truth of the matter and you are now a criminal."

"Oh, my goodness sakes alive!" Ophelia cried. "What a mess you've gotten me in."

"I already said I was sorry."

Ophelia looked up at him. "Do you really think we can cover our tracks and get clean away from Kilpatrick and a posse?"

Bruin knew what the poor girl needed to hear. "I sure do."

"All right," Ophelia sighed, then squared her narrow shoulders. "Let's get out of Prescott as fast as we can."

"Damn good idea," Bruin muttered as he picked up the lead rope and hurried on down the dark and littered back alley with every hope of finding a horse and an extra saddle to steal.

TEN

. ———m———

BRUIN HAD NO trouble finding a couple of horses tied in
front of a saloon. He stripped the saddle off one for himself,
and led the better of the two around back in the alley where
Ophelia was anxiously waiting.

"Why'd you pick such a big horse for me?" she complained. "Why, he's almost as tall as your ugly mule."

"That just means he has long legs and can run faster."

"And he's white."

"For your information, it's a mare and she's a palomino,"
Bruin said as he struggled to lengthen the stirrups on his saddle. He let them down as far as they would go, but they'd still
be a mite too short. "Ophelia, go ahead and mount that mare
and I'll adjust your stirrups."

Ophelia climbed onto the palomino and the mare reared,
almost throwing her off its back. Bruin grabbed the mare's ear
and twisted it like a wet dishrag. The animal tried to paw him
with a foreleg, but Bruin threw his shoulder into the mare, almost knocking her over sideways.

"Are you crazy!" Ophelia screeched. "I'm not riding this wild thing."

"Oh, yes, you are," Bruin said, releasing the animal's leg and then its ear. "And she's just had a lesson in manners so she'll be good now. It's a damn shame the way the cowboys of today let their horses turn rank."

Ophelia said, "Let's stop talking and get out of here. I just hope that you weren't bragging when you said that you knew how to hide our tracks. Otherwise, we'll be caught for sure. Don't forget that they hang horse thieves in Arizona."

"They wouldn't hang you," Bruin said as he climbed on Maggot's back and grabbed his reins. "Probably just shoot you instead."

Ophelia said something, but Bruin was already sending his mule up the alley at a fast trot. The palomino mare followed, and when Bruin saw Ophelia bouncing up and down like a trout bobber on fast-running stream, he said, "Don't you even know how to ride?"

"I never had the money for a damned horse! This thing is already killing me."

As they reached the outskirts of town, Bruin forced Maggot into a gallop. The Missouri mule hated to run, and it laid its ears back like a jackrabbit facing a hard wind. But they were moving fast now, and when Bruin glanced back over his shoulder, he could see Ophelia hanging onto her saddle horn for dear life.

She's going to be all blistered up in a couple of hours and it's going to be hell on her, he thought. *But it'll be a whole lot worse on the both of us if the marshal and his posse catch us tomorrow.*

BRUIN MEANT TO make the most of what little of the night they had left. Most fugitives running from the law would have cut a straight line across the country . . . one easy to read and follow. Bruin, however, chose to stay on the main road leading north, and he was surprised at how many wagons there were traveling at this early hour. Furthermore, he saw camps of men every few miles although most of them were not yet stirring.

Not wanting to attract any more attention than they were already getting, Bruin asked, "Ophelia, what in tarnation is going on here?"

"They're building a railroad from Prescott up to the Santa Fe main line at Seligman. The town has been raising money like crazy for months in order to get the three hundred thousand dollars needed to lay track over seventy-five miles."

"What do they want a train to go down to Prescott for?"

"They say that it will keep our capital in town. The people down in Tucson are trying to take it away."

"Prescott should let Tucson have the capital, which will just attract a bunch of government leeches."

"Being the territorial capital is a great source of pride to Prescott. It brings lots of business to our town."

"Humph!" Bruin snorted. "I never even had the time to file my mining claim with our territorial government. And now, of course, I'm bound to be hanged if I ever return to make my claim legal. Ophelia, do you have any idea what that means?"

"No."

"It means," Bruin continued, "that anyone fast enough with a gun or sneaky enough with a rifle can follow me into the Superstition Mountains and kill me for my gold strike. After that, all they'd have to do is to legally file it back in Prescott."

"Then you should stay away from your gold mine for a while. Besides, you need to remember that I didn't give Marshal Kilpatrick all of that gold in your pouch."

"How much did you keep?" Bruin asked with sudden interest. "We are going to need traveling money."

"I kept it *all*," Ophelia replied, looking quite pleased.

Bruin reined Maggot up short. "How did you do that? Don't tell me that Marshal Kilpatrick was too stupid not to take a peek into that pouch during your poor mother's funeral."

"Oh, Kilpatrick looked, all right."

"Then?"

Ophelia was more than happy to explain. "My teacher and best friend had some fool's gold stuffed in a jar on her bookshelf. It was as much her idea as mine to switch that jar of fool's gold for your real stuff. Bruin, didn't you even know about fool's gold?"

"Oh, I know about it," he replied. "Being a prospector, I've seen my share and can recognize it pretty quick. But you and your teacher were right . . . most men can't tell the difference at a glance."

"Well, then," Ophelia said, "you ought to be proud of me for fooling Marshal Kilpatrick."

"I am! But it'll make him all the more determined to ride us down and skin us alive . . . before he hangs us from a tree limb."

They rode north in silence and as the eastern sky began to lighten, Bruin could see camps of railroad workers stirring awake for breakfast.

"Those fellas are sure up early," Bruin observed. "They must be in an awful hurry to build your town's railroad."

"They are," Ophelia assured him as a wagon load of construction workers passed them in the semidarkness. "If the railroad isn't finished by December 31, there will be a one-thousand-dollar-a-mile penalty."

"Are you serious?"

"I am," Ophelia insisted. "And I'm also wondering why we are following this road where everyone can see us when we ought to be cutting across country."

"It's because a posse can't follow our tracks if they've been walked over by other horses or run over by the wheels of wagons. The thing is, Ophelia, a mule like Maggot lays down a different kind of track than a common horse. It'd be easy to pick up Maggot's hoofprints out on open land, but I'm hoping they'll be covered up good by the time that Kilpatrick can form a posse and start his chase."

"I hope you're right."

"We'll hit a river or at least a creek pretty soon. When we

do, we'll leave this road and follow the water wherever it goes. That will throw off anyone following us."

IT WAS LATE even for Marshal Kilpatrick when he arrived at his office that morning. He had enjoyed a long and leisurely breakfast, and was balancing a cup of steaming coffee in his left hand while juggling his keys in his right hand. The coffee slurped over the side of his cup and scalded his hand.

"Damn!" he shouted, dropping the cup and then twisting the key hard.

The door slammed open under the force of his foot. Kilpatrick glanced around to see if anyone had noticed his clumsiness, and saw an old drunk named Pete smirking. Pete had been a town mainstay for years. A former town merchant and prosperous man, Pete had turned to liquor when his wife and child had died of a mysterious fever. Now, he just spent his days and nights drinking, but he didn't bother anyone, and in fact was quite popular among the townspeople. He had a dry sense of humor and a ready smile for women and children of all ages.

"You got something to say, Pete?" Kilpatrick challenged, so angry that he wanted to strike out and hurt the old man.

"No, sir," the drunk replied, wiping the grin off his face with a dirty sleeve.

"Then get on your way, you worthless old sot, or I'll throw you in the cell with that giant I've got locked up."

Pete grinned. "I doubt you could do that, Marshal."

Kilpatrick had a mind to run over and smack Pete across the side of the head with his revolver, but he was already halfway inside his office, so he dismissed the man and kicked the door shut in his wake.

He placed the empty mug on a counter and, still not looking toward the cell, called, "Well, Bruin Henry, I expect you are really thirsty now. I'd brought a cup of coffee for you but it spilled. Too bad. Maybe I'll bring you some water later if you've got some gold hidden."

Kilpatrick finally turned toward the cell, and that's when his morning got even worse, because the cell door was wide open and his prisoner was gone. Kilpatrick couldn't believe his eyes. He gaped, then staggered toward the cell. He even dashed inside it and kicked the mattress to make sure his prisoner wasn't hiding. Then he turned, and finally noticed that one of the massive cell bars was bent like a bowstring.

"Damnation!" he shouted, grabbing the offending bar and trying to tear it completely free. But the bar wouldn't budge no matter how hard the marshal of Prescott swore and wrenched at it with all his considerable might.

Kilpatrick drew his gun and ran back outside as if he might catch his escaped prisoner standing on the street corner. But the only one standing on the corner was Pete the drunk, almost bent over double and howling with crazy laughter.

Something terrible arose in Kilpatrick and he ran across the street consumed by a red rage. Before Pete could retreat, Kilpatrick pistol-whipped him so hard across the forehead that his skull split open like an overripe melon. Pete's bloodshot eyes rolled up in his head and blood gushed from his nose and forehead as he collapsed, quivering and moaning.

I've killed him, the marshal thought, panic rising as he glanced wildly around and realized that there were a few witnesses. *I've killed this drunken sot and now there will be hell to pay. Pete was a nuisance, but he was harmless and popular.*

Several of the witnesses turned and hurried away, afraid of Kilpatrick. But a few others gathered in a cluster, and the marshal could see that one of them was the town's outspoken editor, Mr. J. D. Hadley.

"He's all right!" Kilpatrick shouted without sounding at all convincing. "Pete is all right!"

But the editor and a few other influential men of the town weren't convinced. One of them hurried off to find a doctor, and Hadley came over to kneel beside the dying drunk. The editor felt for a pulse, found none, and then looked Kilpatrick square in the eye.

"You've killed him," he said, voice hard and unforgiving.

"We saw you run over here and pistol-whip this man without any reason, and now Pete is dead!"

"He . . . he set my prisoner free!"

Hadley scoffed. "Pete?"

"That's right!"

"Nonsense," Hadley challenged.

"If you don't believe me, go look in at my jail cell"

But Hadley shook his head. "I don't believe you, Marshal. Not for one minute do I believe you. And even if Pete did help the prisoner escape, what you did to him just now was still a terrible murder."

Kilpatrick backed away from the dead man and the others, who were glaring at him. "Listen," he blurted out. "Pete wasn't as harmless as he looked. I have evidence that he—"

"Stop it!" the outraged editor shouted, coming to his feet. "You murdered this poor old drunk in front of me and plenty of other witnesses. Marshal Kilpatrick, by all that I stand for and that is holy, justice is about to be done. I've been aware of your temper and viciousness for a good long time now, as have others on the town council. I'm calling a meeting within the hour and you will be arrested."

Something hard rose up in Kilpatrick's throat, as it had all his life when he was backed into a corner. "Oh, yeah, *who* will arrest me? You?" He sneered. "J. D., if you cause me trouble, I swear that I'll kill you."

The town's editor paled, but when he spoke, there was still resolve in his voice. "You *will* be arrested and charged with murder."

And then, before Kilpatrick could muster up an answer, the editor and his friends hurried away.

They'll fire me and form up their own posse to arrest me. I can't stand up against all of them. I'm finished in Prescott because of that damned Pete. No, the one I really owe all this misery to is Bruin Henry. And by all that is in me, I swear that I'll track him down and make him pay for this if it's the last thing I ever do!

And I'll do it using his pouch of gold.

ELEVEN

———⚏———

IT WAS LATE in the afternoon when Ophelia cried, "Bruin, the inside of my legs and my backside are on fire! I can't ride this horse another step."

Bruin drew rein and studied the inhospitable terrain. "We don't have any food or water and we can't stop out here on this dry mesa. We have no choice but to ride on until we can find a good place to rest."

"But . . ."

"There's no help for it!" Bruin snapped, more angry at himself for putting the girl in this bad fix than at her for whining. "We're bound to find someone who has some bear or axle grease."

"I'm not putting any bear or axle grease on my blisters."

"Then I'll put it on for you," Bruin told his granddaughter. "We have to keep moving, and there's no choice but to grease you up like a pig and keep riding until we are sure we aren't being chased by a posse from Prescott."

Tears welled up in Ophelia's blue eyes, and the sight of them almost ripped Bruin's heart to shreds. Kicking Maggot harder than he should have, he sent the mule forward, its ears pinned back to its ugly head.

"Sorry about that," Bruin mumbled under his breath to his best friend. "You owe me one for that unkindness."

In reply, Maggot tightened his long ears back harder and snapped his yellow teeth a time or two, letting Bruin know that he was greatly displeased both with the hard pace they'd been setting and with his boot heels.

IT TOOK THEM another hour to find three drifters camped by a tiny spring surrounded by a lush halo of grass. When the men saw Bruin and Ophelia approaching, they waved them in and made it clear that they were welcome to join them under a grove of trees.

"Much obliged," Bruin said, taking their measure and not feeling too comfortable. They looked lean and hard, the kind of men that were always looking to get something for nothing, and he guessed they were a father and his two sons.

"Climb down and loosen your cinches."

But Bruin decided that this camp was unsafe, so he said, "We'll just water our mounts and ride on."

"What about me!" Ophelia cried.

"What's wrong with her?" one of the men asked, sounding more curious than concerned.

"She's got saddle blisters," Bruin answered. "Have you any grease we could buy?"

The three exchanged glances, and Bruin heard one of them mutter something under his breath before he looked up, smiled disarmingly, and said, "Sure we do."

Bruin steered Maggot over to the spring's seep and let the mule paw a hole that quickly filled with water. The mule drank in great noisy gulps that seemed never to stop. When it finally had its fill, Bruin reined Maggot away so that the palomino mare could also quench her thirst.

"That's some mule you're riding, old-timer," the youngest of the strangers said. "Born and bred in Missouri, ain't he?"

"Yep."

Bruin had not turned his back on the three men, and the more he studied their camp, the more he wanted to move along as soon as possible.

"Where you headed?" the oldest asked.

Bruin shrugged. "Just headed east. We'll be moving on as soon as you give me some grease. How much you want for it?"

The oldest one ignored his question. "What's your big hurry?"

Bruin laid his right hand on his hip near his gun and said, "My father told me that time is the most important thing we have and that it's never to be wasted."

The man laughed. "Mister, are you some kind of philosopher?"

"Nope," Bruin replied. "Now, how about that grease for her blisters?"

"You're not only in a hurry, but you're kind of unfriendly," the man said with the friendliness draining from his angular face. He glanced at his sons, who nodded in agreement, then turned back to Bruin. "Why don't you and that girl dismount and have some coffee and beans? Then we'll talk about price and she can salve her blistered little bottom."

Both sons smirked and thought that the remark was funny. But Bruin thought otherwise. He could see that Ophelia's cheeks were burning with indignation. Bruin was now certain that this was a bad bunch already plotting evil designs on him and Ophelia.

"We'll just ride on," he said, wanting to slap the smirk off their faces. "You boys have a good day."

"Grandpa, I just can't ride any farther! My skin is on fire and I'm half starved and thirsty."

"Sure you are, honey," the oldest son told her. "Just get down off that palomino and come on over to rest beside our fire. Coffee, grease, and beans. We'll fix you up just fine. Your grandpa is a hard man, but we're forgiving of his bad manners."

Ophelia actually started to dismount. Hell, she would have dismounted if Bruin hadn't drove Maggot into her mare and then grabbed her arm squeezing it hard.

"Ouch!" she cried. "Bruin, you're hurting me!"

"Let loose of that girl!" one of the men shouted, reaching for his gun.

Bruin did let loose of Ophelia and went for his pistol. A bullet whip-cracked past his face an instant before Bruin's own weapon fired. His bullet struck the youngest man in the chest and knocked him into his father, spoiling the older man's draw. Bruin's second shot was hurried and wild, but his third bullet tore into the older son's leg right above the knee. It knocked him down, and he rolled over and over on the dry leaves screaming.

"Hold it!" Bruin shouted at the father, who now reaching for a shotgun. He was slow, and when he started to raise the weapon, Bruin took aim and yelled, "Drop it or I'll drill you through the gizzard!"

But the man was insane with grief. "You just killed my boy Johnny and shot Bertram in the leg! He's bleeding to death."

Bruin cocked back the hammer of his gun. "Bertram is going to need your help. Better think this out and use your head."

But the old man was too far gone in the head to reason. He threw the shotgun to his shoulder so that Bruin had no choice but to shoot him in the head.

"Grandpa, look out!" Ophelia shouted.

A fourth man appeared from the woods with a rifle. Maybe he'd been out hunting deer or elk, but now he was determined to kill Bruin. His rifle cracked, and a bullet struck Bruin's saddle horn and ricocheted a bloody furrow across the top of Maggot's neck. The big mule squealed and bucked sending Bruin high into the air. He landed on a bed of dead leaves and his gun went flying.

The rifleman fired again, and Bruin rolled knowing that he was as good as dead. The rifleman swept past Ophelia and ran up to stand just a few feet from Bruin, who was disarmed and helpless. The man levered a bullet into the breech and pointed it at Bruin's belly.

"Old man, I'm going to shoot you in the guts so you die slow for what you just did to my pa and my brothers!"

Bruin swallowed hard knowing that there wasn't a thing he could do to save his life. He didn't even have his hunting knife, not that it would have done him any good. But neither Bruin nor the rifleman saw Ophelia pull a derringer out of her frayed dress and jump from the palomino.

"Freeze!" she cried, running up behind the rifleman, who stiffened, then turned around slowly, fists still locked on his Winchester.

Bruin could see the derringer shaking in Ophelia's clenched fist. She held it up close and stuttered, "Drop . . . drop the rifle, mister. I *really* don't want to shoot you."

"Girl, that big sonofabitch you're riding with just killed my whole family. I got to make him pay."

"I won't let you execute Bruin Henry," Ophelia said between her clenched teeth. "This derringer is loaded and I'll use it if I must."

He was the tallest man in his family, and had the cold and merciless eyes of a lobo wolf. Bruin knew that he wouldn't hesitate to kill Ophelia given half a chance. "Ophelia, shoot him!"

But she didn't seem to hear Bruin. "Mister, *please* drop the rifle."

The man took a half step toward Ophelia, but she retreated keeping a small distance between them. "Mister, you do as I say!"

"Ophelia, shoot him now!"

The man swung his rifle and its barrel struck Ophelia in the arm. The derringer discharged harmlessly, and Ophelia tripped on a branch and fell over backward.

The rifleman twisted around to see Bruin rising from the thick carpet of dead leaves, his face a mask of rage. The man tried to get the rifle up and pointed at Bruin's belly, but failed as he was struck in the face with a sledgehammer-like blow.

Bruin landed on the man with drawn-up knees. The rifle was knocked aside, and the man grabbed Bruin's beard and tried to put a thumb in his eyes. Their bodies locked and rolled over and over in the leaves. They punched, bit, and struck at each other again and again, until Bruin got a headlock on the younger man and wrenched his neck back and forth so violently that it finally snapped. The rifleman's back arched for a moment before he went limp. "Grandpa, you killed him!"

"That's right," Bruin admitted before he slowly climbed to his feet, then staggered over to examine Maggot's creased neck.

The mule bit Bruin on the side, just under the ribs. Bruin let out a holler and jumped back. He lifted his shirt and saw blood oozing around the marks of the mule's teeth.

"Why'd he do that to you?" Ophelia asked, jaw hanging open. "You love that ugly mule."

"He's still mad at me for booting him in the ribs last night," Bruin said, not angry at all. "And then getting creased by that bullet didn't help. Maggot just feels that he owed me one."

Ophelia shook her head, then leaned heavily against a tree. She stared at the carnage and shook her head as if she might erase a nightmare. "I can't believe what just happened. I have never seen so many dead men."

Bruin wasn't listening as he went over to see the man he'd wounded in the leg. The man was dead, and Bruin figured that his bullet must have cut through an artery in order for him to bleed out so fast.

Four dead men. What a hell of a waste.

He rejoined Ophelia. "They're all goners."

She studied him intently, and then she shot back, "I guess they're nothing more than just four more notches on your bloody gun."

"I don't keep notches on my gun or my rifle, Ophelia."

She had begun to shake, and was furious. "And I'll bet you don't lose any sleep over what just happened here today!"

"Would you rather *we* were dead?"

"No," Ophelia whispered, sinking down against the trunk of the tree and looking desolated. "But I sure am tired of everyone dying."

"It's a hard world," Bruin explained. "Good people like your mother die young and for no just cause. Old people like myself who have killed plenty of others sometimes die at ninety in their sleep. There's no rhyme or reason to any of it, so you're better off not to even try to figure it out."

"But . . . but if there's really a God in heaven, how can he . . ." Ophelia shook her head, tears welling up in her eyes.

"How can he allow so much death and injustice? Ophelia, I don't know the answer and nobody else . . . not even a preacher . . . does either. Maybe you'll learn the answer to those kind of questions from old St. Peter when you get to the Pearly Gates. But until then, the only thing we can do is just to try to stay alive."

"We were very, very lucky."

"Luck has something to do with it, but not all."

"You're old, but you shoot straight and fast."

"I do," he agreed. "But I'm not nearly as good with a gun as your father."

Ophelia look drained and shattered. A long time passed before she said, "Grandpa, do you think they have any grease for my blisters?"

"I don't know. I'll see what I can find."

"Never mind." Ophelia went to catch up the palomino. "All I want is to get as far away from here as I can as quickly as possible."

Bruin understood that. He went to collect any cash that the dead men were carrying. Then, he'd pack up things and they'd keep moving until dark, provided he could find some liniment or grease for Ophelia's blisters. It was a sad and sorry state of affairs when a girl like that had to see so much blood and dying.

Still, if they ever found Link Cochran, Bruin reckoned she'd see at least one more man die, and it would probably be himself.

TWELVE

—⁂—

EX-MARSHAL WADE KILPATRICK knew that he had very little time to gather his personal belongings and get out of Prescott. Kilpatrick thought that it was a damn dirty shame the way that town editor J. D. Hadley and his blowhard cronies had just happened to be watching when he pistol-whipped that old drunk just a little bit too hard. But hell, old Pete hadn't been worth anything. He'd been a bother and a nuisance and was better off dead.

As soon as the editor and his friends had marched off to call their town council meeting, Kilpatrick hurried into his marshal's office, where he quickly collected a pair of extra Colt revolvers, a good lever-action Winchester, and a scarred but large-bore hunting rifle with a scope. He also pocketed three boxfuls of ammunition and a few dollars he kept hidden in his desk as emergency money. He took these possessions over to the livery stable and yelled for the owner to show his ugly face.

"Eli, I'll need my horse saddled and ready to ride," he said in a terse voice to the liveryman. "I'll also need a packhorse and I want a good one . . . not some plug that will go lame ten miles from town."

"I got a roan mule that will go as far and fast as your saddle horse," Eli said. "But a pack mule is worthless without a packsaddle and good lead rope."

"How much are you asking for everything?"

The liveryman screwed up his face to make it appear that he was trying his best to come up with a fair price. Kilpatrick had no time for such nonsense and yelled, "How much, dammit!"

"Fifty dollars!" Eli cried, taking a step back and then whining, "Marshal, even at that I'm losing—"

Kilpatrick knew that he was being gouged hard, but there was no time to dicker with this man, so he reluctantly agreed to what he thought was an outrageous price.

"All right," he growled. "I'll pay you in gold nuggets when I come back in a few minutes. Have both animals ready. Put these pistols and boxes of ammunition in my saddlebags and find a couple of scabbards for the rifles."

"Marshal, you sure are in a hurry. No disrespect intended, but I'd say that you almost look like a man who's just seen a ghost."

"If you don't start moving and quit standing here, then I expect you'll be the one seeing ghosts. Now step lively!"

"Yes, sir!" Eli replied. "I expect you're going after whoever stole that big white mule."

Kilpatrick had turned and was striding out the door when he froze in his tracks. "The Missouri mule was stolen?"

"Yes, sir! Late last night."

"Bruin Henry must have took him."

"I don't think so, Marshal."

Kilpatrick glanced sharply at the man. "Why the hell not?"

"Because I can read tracks pretty good, and whoever took the mule had real small feet. Sure wasn't that giant you had in your jail."

Kilpatrick frowned. He had just assumed that Bruin Henry had escaped by using his incredible strength to somehow find a weakness in the jail bars that allowed him to finally bend one of them enough to squeeze his way out to freedom. But now, this stupid liveryman was telling him that Bruin Henry had had help.

"Did you wipe out the tracks?"

"Well, I didn't see 'em right away and lost a few, but there are some still visible. Want to see 'em?"

"I sure do," Kilpatrick said despite the fact that he was in a huge hurry.

"There they are," the liveryman said a moment later. "Mighty small feet for a man."

Kilpatrick shook his head. "It wasn't a man that made those tracks. It was that damned Ophelia Cochran!"

"Are you sure?"

"Of course I am! Who else would steal Henry's white mule?"

Eli said something else, but Kilpatrick was already gone. He made straight for the alley behind his jail, almost certain what he'd find, and he wasn't disappointed.

"It was the girl, all right," he muttered to himself, thinking about how she'd been so compliant yesterday at her mother's funeral. And all the while she'd been planning to steal the Missouri mule and use it to help her grandfather escape. Well, he'd make her pay just the same as that old man.

Having confirmed his suspicions, Kilpatrick hurried over to the little house on South Granite that he rented for twenty dollars a month. He'd planned to buy the house, renovate it himself, and then think about taking himself a wife and maybe running for the office of mayor. The widow woman he'd planned to marry wasn't much to look at . . . in fact she was downright homely . . . but her husband had left her with a large bank account. Homely, stingy, and not much fun, she would have been easy pickings. He'd planned to marry her and, in a few years, attend her funeral. He'd not worked out how Mabel would have a fatal accident, but he'd have thought of something before she drove him crazy with her nagging and petty ways.

In the meantime, he'd enjoyed a prostitute named Delia
O'Dell, who worked at the Wild Mustang Club and who was
everything Mabel wasn't, except that she was always spend-
ing more money than she could earn on her backside. He'd
miss Delia very much, but there was nothing to say that he
couldn't came back for her after things had settled down. J. D.
Hadley and his cronies would soon lose interest in the death
of a common drunk, and by then, Kilpatrick figured he would
have tracked down Bruin and Ophelia and made them reveal
where that gold mine was in the Superstition Mountains.

Everything is going to work out for the best, he thought,
gathering up his personal belongings and piling them all on
his bed ready to be stuffed into a canvas sack that he could tie
to the back of his saddle. He also rolled up a couple of blankets and a heavy canvas coat that would keep him dry in even
the heaviest downpour. It would have been nice to have gone
to the general store and provisioned himself with canned
goods, but at least he had two bottles of decent whiskey to
take along on such short notice.

Kilpatrick pulled out his pocket watch. It had been over an
hour since he'd cracked old Pete's skull with his pistol. Why,
the town of Prescott owed him a reward for ridding its good
citizens of that old reprobate. But instead, the editor and city
council would be meeting right now. They'd quickly pass a
formal resolution to terminate his employment, and then
they'd start wrangling about how to arrest him for murder.

Hellfire, he thought, there wasn't a man in this town stupid
enough to brace Wade Kilpatrick with a gun and try to put
him in jail. But then, if the price were right, Kilpatrick figured
that enough men could be hurriedly gathered to surround and
arrest him. And that was why he had to leave this town in a
hurry.

Kilpatrick was almost ready to go. He lifted a dirty rug and
pried up a floorboard where he kept his stash of money and
Bruin Henry's pouch of gold, which he'd taken from Ophelia
at the funeral.

Kilpatrick bounced the heavy gold pouch up and down in

the palm of his hand. *This will take me as far as I need to go to find the old prospector and that ragged orphan. It will take me to wherever in the Superstition Mountains this came from and make me rich. Everything is finally working out for the best. I couldn't have planned it any better.*

He shoved the pouch of gold in his pocket, shouldered his canvas bag, and headed out the door.

"Wade?"

He swore to himself and turned. Out of habit, he smiled and said, "Hello, Mabel. How are you doing?"

"I'm not doing well at all," she said, looking highly distressed. "I just learned that you struck with the butt of your gun and killed Pete Olsen."

"Olsen? Was that his full name? I guess I'd forgotten."

"Yes, his name was Peter L. Olsen and he was once a very fine and respectable gentleman before tragedy turned him toward the bottle."

"Well, we all have our problems. I guess Peter just wasn't man enough to stand up to his pain cold sober."

Mabel was in her late thirties, but she looked ten years older. Small and plump, she had flabby arms, a double chin, bags under both of her now-misty eyes. "Wade, did you really strike that old man and kill him?"

"I did," he replied. "And now I'm leaving Prescott, so if you'll excuse me . . ."

But she didn't move to allow him to pass in the hallway. "Why?" she demanded, looking hurt and confused. "Mr. Olsen was harmless."

"And useless." Kilpatrick had been nice too long to this pitiful creature he'd planned to marry and then dispose of for her money, and his smile was replaced by a hard expression loaded with contempt. "Get out of my way, Mabel. I'm in a hurry."

"You *shouldn't* have killed Mr. Olsen. There was no earthly reason to do a cruel thing like that. I know being a marshal is not easy and demands a certain amount of toughness, but Wade, I certainly didn't think you were that kind of a man."

"You have no idea what kind of a man I really am," he said harshly. "And do you want to know why?"

She shrank back and actually shook her head. For the first time, she looked afraid.

"I'll tell you why, Mabel. You don't know me because all you do is talk about yourself. You just talk, talk, talk! You're a damned empty-headed magpie and I've long hated the very sight of you. The idea of climbing into bed with an ugly little cow like you has always made me want to empty my guts."

Mabel's eyes widened and her hand flew to her mouth. "I know you're a hard man, but you can soften with the love of God and . . . and I am in love with you, Wade."

"Then the joke is on you," he said, grabbing her by the shoulder and slamming her against the wall a moment before he passed.

The house was surrounded by a white picket fence desperately in need of fresh paint. Kilpatrick almost tore its flimsy gate off its post in leaving.

"Wade! Don't leave me. I'll stand by you through this to the end. Please don't run from your troubles."

"I'm running, all right, and I'm glad it's you I'm putting behind!"

Mabel sobbed, and then screamed, "Wade, you're no good!"

He laughed, making a cruel, guttural sound. "You're wrong, because I'm real good. Better than you could have ever imagined . . . better than you could have *survived*. I'd have killed you on our wedding night, but at least you'd have died with a smile on your ugly puss!"

Somehow, he knew she had collapsed by the gate. He could hear her sobbing all the way down Granite, and he didn't give a damn. In fact, Kilpatrick was feeling pretty good about things when he returned to the livery still bouncing the pouch of gold in his left hand.

"Are we saddled and ready?" he asked.

"Yes, sir. I couldn't find a scabbard big enough for the hunting rifle so I rigged up some grain sacks. Doubled them up and cut holes in them to drape over your saddle horn."

Kilpatrick was not pleased when he saw the arrangement. "Dammit, Eli. I'll look like some kind of idiot with my rifle in a grain sack! Is that really the best you can do for me?"

"I'm afraid so. But look at this mule. Finest jenny I've had in many a day."

The mule was smallish, but Kilpatrick was a good enough judge of livestock to see that she had an excellent conformation. Good head, intelligence instead of stubbornness in the eyes, straight legs.

"She'll do," he said, tossing his canvas bag over the pack-saddle and tying it down securely. He then checked his cinch and made a quick all-around inspection. "I guess I'm ready."

"I hope you find Bruin Henry and that girl."

"I will."

"You gonna bring them both back for a trial?"

"Expect so." In truth, Kilpatrick knew that he would leave no witnesses in the Superstition Mountains.

"Well, Marshal. I'm glad that I have been able to serve you today. Now all that is required is the fifty dollars and . . . oh, I'm afraid that you are a month behind on your livery bill. So the total comes to fifty-seven dollars. It would normally be sixty dollars, but since you're the marshal, you get a special rate."

Eli wrung his hands together and waited, looking nervous and expectant.

Kilpatrick had an almost overwhelming urge to crack two skulls on the same morning. It would be so easy.

"I wish you the best of luck on your manhunt," Eli blurted out. "The town will hail you a hero when you return with that pair."

"Yeah," Kilpatrick agreed, wondering how this idiot could have failed to hear about the death of Pete Olsen. Or perhaps he had heard and that was why he was starting to sweat even though it was cool inside this ramshackle livery barn.

"Just fifty-seven dollars, Marshal Kilpatrick. It's not much to ask for a good mule and packsaddle even without your livery bill."

"I guess . . . I guess it isn't," Kilpatrick heard himself say as he reached into his pocket for the pouch containing his gold nuggets.

He put his fingers into the pouch and felt around a moment, watching the liveryman's eyes fix on the pouch with anticipation. "Here, Eli. This nugget is worth at least sixty."

He placed the small nugget in Eli's palm then started to mount his horse.

"Marshal!"

"Yeah."

"Uhh . . . this is fool's gold."

Kilpatrick had one boot in the stirrup when he was hit with this news. For a moment, he hung on the side of his horse, and then he lowered himself to the powdery earthen barn floor.

"What did you say?" he asked softly.

The liveryman's hand was shaking so hard he had to close his fingers over the nugget. "I . . . I bit it and it's hard. Can't be gold. I'm sorry, but it just isn't anything but fool's gold."

Kilpatrick's own hand shot out and his fingernails dug deeply into Eli's wrist. The smaller man cried out in pain and the nugget was exposed. Kilpatrick snatched it up and bit it like a piece of peppermint. It almost broke his tooth.

"Fool's gold." He spat it out, and the worthless piece of rock struck Eli in the face. Kilpatrick tore open Bruin's leather pouch and poured a torrent of nuggets into the palm of his own hand. He stared at them and, as if they were candy, he began to bite down on them one at a time. And after each was sampled, he spat it at Eli.

"I'm sorry, Marshal. I'm real sorry, but I think I'd rather just have cash. No offense, you understand. It's just that . . ."

Consumed by a towering rage born of trickery, Kilpatrick hurled the remaining nuggets into the man's face so hard that Eli cried out and bowed his head.

"Don't kill me!" he shouted, staggering backward and then

falling across a huge pile of manure that he gathered, and added to first thing every morning before breakfast. "It's not my fault that it's fool's gold!"

Kilpatrick took a step toward the man with his gun coming into his hand. Eli screeched and scrambled over the pile of horse manure and disappeared down the other side.

"You're not worth killing," Kilpatrick said as he slammed his boot into his stirrup and then hauled himself into his saddle. He grabbed the jenny's lead rope and headed for the north side of town.

"I'm coming after you," he repeated again and again as he left Prescott behind. "And when I find you . . . I'll make you both wish you had never been born."

THIRTEEN

—⚬—

"BRUIN, THERE'S A town up ahead and I'm not riding any farther," Ophelia said. "These last three days have been the worst in my life."

Her eyes filled with tears. "First Mother dies, then I commit the crime of breaking you out of jail . . ."

"Yes," Bruin corrected, "but not without Maggot's considerable help."

"So what! They won't throw that ugly mule in prison when we're caught by Marshal Kilpatrick and his men."

"I guess not," Bruin conceded.

"And after I broke you out of jail we killed four men! Four!"

"I killed them," Bruin said. "You had nothing to do with it."

Ophelia dried her eyes on her sleeve. "I don't know why I chose to get into all this trouble. I could have stayed in Prescott with my friend the schoolteacher.

"You did it because I'm your grandfather."

"Wrong! I did it because I knew that Marshal Kilpatrick

was vicious and that he would probably kill you, which you *do* deserve."

Bruin shrugged. "If you're so sure I deserve to die, then why'd you go and bother to help bust me out of jail?"

"Because Kilpatrick is evil and he was torturing you," Ophelia said. "And two wrongs don't make a right. And besides, I promised my mother on her deathbed that I'd do what I could for you and then find my father."

"Well," Bruin said, trying to hide his disappointment. "I'm glad that you're at least keeping your promise to Kate. I'm doing the same thing by agreeing to try to find your father even though we have sworn to kill each other on sight."

"I doubt he'll just shoot you down," Ophelia said, "even though you are a wanted man and a cold-blooded killer."

Bruin really wanted to tell his granddaughter that, when it came to cold-blooded killers, her father was without equal. But he knew she'd not believe him, so he just kept his mouth shut and rode on. And although he didn't want to admit it, he was plenty ready to stop and rest, have a good meal and make sure that their animals were heavily grained, and fed all the hay they could stomach. The last few days had been hard on both him and Ophelia. It was no good when you had to keep looking over your back all the time, every minute expecting to get shot by the law.

So far, though, he'd seen no signs of Kilpatrick or a posse on their tail. Perhaps he really had managed to throw them off and they'd given up the pursuit. Still, Bruin prided himself on being an excellent judge of men, even though he had done his best to avoid them for many years. Marshal Kilpatrick was vicious and prideful. Not only would he have been shamed by the escape and damage to his jail cell, but when he discovered that Ophelia had tricked him with a pouch full of fool's gold, the man would be livid with rage and bent on revenge.

"What's the name of that town up ahead?" she asked.

"It's Flagstaff and it's a timber and railroad town. It has way too many people."

"That may be true, but perhaps my father will be there."

"I wouldn't count on it," Bruin told her. "For all we know, he could be anywhere between California and New York City. Might be in New Orleans or up in Alaska. A man like that travels fast and light in order to stay one step ahead of the trouble he's made."

"What trouble? Don't forget that my father is a United States marshal. All we should have to do is find one of those fellas and then ask him where my father has been assigned by Washington, D.C."

"That's it, huh?"

"Yes." Ophelia stood up in her stirrups. "I don't think I'll be able to sit down for a week. If we hadn't come across that traveling drummer and bought that medicinal liniment I'd never have made it this far."

"Sure you would of," Bruin argued. "You do what you have to in this world to stay alive."

"That's what Mother used to say about the painted women in Prescott. She was always kind and polite to them, even though many respectable women were not."

"Your mother was too good for this world," Bruin said, his voice rough with emotion. "I feel bad about letting her down the way I did. I should have come to visit a whole lot sooner."

"You only showed up in Prescott to file your mining claim."

"That's true, but I was hoping to see you and Kate."

"I wish I could believe that, but I don't," Ophelia said, quickly looking away.

ENTERING FLAGSTAFF, BRUIN could see that it was exactly the kind of a town he would normally go far out of his way to avoid. At one time it might have been a decent little settlement, but with the coming of the Santa Fe Railroad, Flagstaff had become a boomtown filled with the usual riffraff you'd expect to find when lumberjacks, railroad workers, women of ill repute, and land speculators all came together for quick profit.

"Ophelia, I expect that there will be a marshal's office in a town this large," Bruin said as they started up the main street. "As well as a doctor who can give you better liniment for your saddle sores."

"Where will we stay?" she asked, looking around at all the rough men on the sidewalks.

"You'll need to find a boardinghouse for ladies and I'll pick some fleabag hotel."

"You don't sound too happy."

"I always try to avoid such places as this."

Ophelia was blunt. "No doubt that's because you get drunk and then either beat up or kill people."

Bruin almost smiled. "You must think I'm about the most wicked man in all of Arizona."

"No," she answered. "I think Marshal Kilpatrick is the most wicked. But you're a close second."

As they rode up the main street, Bruin could feel eyes on him and Maggot. It wasn't unexpected, but having so many stare at him and the Missouri mule always made him feel uneasy. He could never be sure that someone hadn't seen him on a wanted poster.

"There's the marshal's office," he said, reining Maggot up to a hitching rail. "Go inside and see if they've heard of Link Cochran."

"*United States Marshal* Link Cochran," Ophelia corrected as she dismounted with not a little discomfort. "Ahh, it sure feels good to stand up."

"I'll water the animals while I wait for you."

Brain took Maggot to the water trough first and let the animal drink its fill, and then he watered the palomino. Several men watched him closely, but when he gave them a menacing scowl, they moved on. There were a dozen saloons in sight, and Bruin would have liked to have wet his whistle, but knew that would be a mistake. Now that he had the responsibility of looking out for his granddaughter, he'd have to be far more careful.

He led their animals over toward a stand of pine trees and

squatted on his heels watching and waiting for Ophelia. A lumberman passed him smoking a cigar, and Bruin asked the man if he had an extra to sell.

"Nope," the lumberman said. "But you can buy 'em all over town."

"How many people live here?"

"A couple of thousand and more arriving every day."

Bruin shook his head. "I never could understand why folks would want to clump up together."

The lumberjack had curly brown hair and a handlebar mustache. Good-looking and of average size, he had friendly eyes when he said, "You strike me as a real loner. If I was a photographer, I'd take your picture riding that huge white mule. A city man like myself doesn't see many the likes of you anymore."

Bruin was not sure if he was being complimented or insulted. "I guess you don't see the likes of me because you never leave this collection of human confusion. But if you took to the hills after wild horses, cattle, or seeking gold, you'd see more country and far more interesting folks."

The man laughed and puffed on his cigar. "I expect you are right. But I'm a railroad mechanic. I work on steam engines and have a bright future with the Santa Fe. What kind of future would I have poking around in the country?"

"A much more interesting one."

The young man chuckled. "You're quick-minded, old-timer. You ever find any gold or wealth in Arizona?"

"I have," Bruin answered, too proud to deny the fact.

"If that's so, then why are you riding that mangy old mule?"

"Son, if you can't appreciate a fine animal like Maggot, then there is no use in my wasting my breath trying to explain." Just then Bruin saw Ophelia emerge from the marshal's office and she wasn't smiling. "It's been nice talking to you, mister. But we have talked enough and now it's time for you to mosey along."

The young railroad mechanic didn't seem offended by

having been dismissed. He headed up the street, still puffing on his cigar and occasionally glancing back at Bruin and his Missouri mule.

"Well," Bruin asked when Ophelia joined him. "What'd you learn from the town marshal?"

"He said that he'd never heard of my father, but when I told him he was a federal lawman, he offered to send a telegraph to the nearest federal office in Denver."

"He'd do that for nothing?"

"No," Ophelia admitted. "I had to pay for the telegraph. The marshal said that the people in Denver would know my father and most likely where he was assigned at the moment."

Bruin would have bet his mule that the people in Denver would never have heard of Link Cochran, but he said, "So how long will this telegraph business take?"

"We should have an answer by five o'clock. If not, then tomorrow morning at the latest."

"Then we need to find a livery, rooms for the night, and a café."

"I expect so."

Bruin could see that something was upsetting Ophelia, and knew it had to be her disappointment at not immediately finding out about her father. He wanted to tell her that she was in for even bigger disappointments in the days, weeks, and perhaps even months to come as they searched for Link. And if they found him, that would be the biggest disappointment of all.

BRUIN HAD NOT slept well that night in Flagstaff. He had no idea if Marshal Kilpatrick was close on their trail with a posse, so he was more than eager to leave town as soon as possible. He expected that Ophelia would be terribly disappointed when she learned that no one in Denver had heard of Link, but that probably wouldn't change her idealized opinion of the man. Nothing was going to convince her of the truth about Link until they met.

Bruin ate an early breakfast on his own, and then he went to the livery and got their animals ready to travel. He'd made sure that both Maggot and the palomino had received double rations of hay and grain, and they looked better for the good feeding.

"You wouldn't be interested in selling that mule, would you?" the liveryman asked as Bruin saddled the ornery beast.

"Nope."

"You don't see them like that much anymore," the man drawled in a voice that told Bruin he was born and raised in the South. "That is the biggest, ugliest mule I've come across in all my years."

"Thank you."

"Bruin?"

He turned to see Ophelia. "How you doing?"

"I'm all right. I went to the doctor this morning and he gave me some medicinal liniment for my saddle sores. He said I shouldn't ride in a saddle for a week or more."

Bruin frowned. "We can't stay here that long for reasons I'm sure you understand."

"No," she agreed, "we can't. But since I can't ride a horse for a while, I was thinking that we ought to buy a buggy and hitch up your mule."

"What!"

She folded her arms across her chest and planted her feet solidly on the dusty floor. "You heard me. Mules pull things. We can afford a buggy, so why not throw our saddles and gear into a buckboard or buggy and ride in comfort?"

Bruin took her arm and led her away from the liveryman, whose head was bobbing in agreement. No doubt the man had a buggy for sale and would like to sell it at great profit.

"Child," Bruin said in a low voice, "where is your mind? Maggot is a *riding* mule and he doesn't pull wagons. Why, he'd be so insulted to be hitched to a wagon that he'd run away with us and cause one helluva wreck! He'd most likely kill himself and us right along with him."

Ophelia made sure that she could not be heard. She leaned

close to Bruin and whispered, "Then we could hitch up the palomino you stole in Prescott."

"Not a good idea."

"Why not!"

"Because we may need to travel fast and over rough ground if Kilpatrick is on our trail."

"Be that as it may . . . I can't sit a horse for at least a week. Why, it's all I can do now not to walk like I've got a big carrot up my backside."

Bruin was shocked. "Don't you talk like that or I'll wash your mouth out with lye soap!"

"Then don't be suggesting we ride."

They stood toe-to-toe, Bruin towering over the girl, but Ophelia was determined to win her point and she would not back down from his glare. Finally, Bruin looked away a moment, then said, "You still haven't told me what you learned from the telegram."

"The people in Denver sent back the message that my father quit the federal government as a United States marshal and they didn't know where he'd gone."

Bruin almost fell over. "The Denver feds had actually heard of him?"

"Yes, and his last assignment was to catch a couple of stagecoach robbers down by a town called Pine River."

"I've heard of it. Pine River is located somewhere up on the Mogollon Rim."

"Well," Ophelia said proudly, "my father caught the stagecoach robbers and took them to Tucson, where they were turned over to the authorities. Then he quit, and that's the last that's been heard of him."

"Are you sure?"

"Here's the telegraph they sent. Can you read?"

"Do cougars crap in the woods? Of course I can read!"

"Then read it for yourself," she ordered, taking the telegram from her pocket and shoving it up into his face.

Bruin did read the telegram, and it actually did say that

Link Cochran had been a federal marshal and that his last assignment was on the Mogollon Rim.

"Well I'll be fried and dyed," he breathed.

"So why don't we buy a buggy and go find him instead of standing here arguing?" Ophelia challenged. "We've got plenty of gold."

"Shhh! Don't ever say that to the person you're about to buy something from."

Ophelia saw his point, but the damage had already been done. The liveryman was licking his lips in anticipation, and Bruin knew they were about to get shafted in the deal.

FOURTEEN

—◆◆◆—

BRUIN WAS IN a dark mood as he and Ophelia passed Fort Tuthill on a deeply rutted road. He held the lines and watched the ears of his mule sway back and forth as the animal moved along harnessed in tandem with the palomino.

"Stop looking so upset," Ophelia said, breaking a long silence. "It will do Maggot good to pull this wagon for a while. Pulling is what mules do best."

"He's never going to forgive me," Bruin lamented. "And I sure don't see why we had to buy this damned medicine wagon!"

"We bought it because it was cheap and in excellent condition. Remember?"

The wagon had been cheap, but only because it was such an eyesore and oddity. The former owner, a fellow who called himself Dr. Good Health, had converted an ordinary buckboard into this monstrosity by hammering together a tall, rectangular box, which he had used as a storehouse; a brewery of his fake medicines and tonics, and sleeping quarters. The box rose to a ridiculous height of about ten feet over the bed of the

buckboard, and it possessed a shingled, pitched roof with a
rusty stovepipe jutting another two feet into the sky.

Not content with having the most top-heavy and foolish
looking wagon in Arizona, Dr. Health had installed a front
and rear door and two side windows with white lace curtains.
The abomination was painted bright red with white windows
and blue doors. And if that wasn't enough to scare any respectable animal that they might encounter on the road, the
ungainly medicine wagon was emblazoned with poorly drawn
figures either drinking Dr. Good Health's tonic or refusing it
with "R.I.P." labeled over their prostrated bodies.

"If a wind comes up, this damned thing is going to flip
over on us," Bruin warned. "And when we come to the first
steep hill, we ain't going to be able to climb it because this
wagon must weigh a thousand pounds."

"You're such a pessimist," Ophelia told him. "The shingled roof is sound and it will serve us well in bad weather.
Furthermore, this medicine wagon has two cots and a little
cooking stove. I think we really got lucky when we bought
this wagon for only a hundred dollars."

"I am nearly mortified at the thought of being seen in such
a rambling woodpile," Bruin groused.

"If that's true, then get set to be mortified," Ophelia told
him. "Because here comes a cavalry patrol."

Bruin handed the reins to his granddaughter. "I'm getting
inside."

"You sit right here!" Ophelia ordered, handing the lines
back to Bruin. "I'm sure that the United States Army and its
brave cavalrymen have better things to do with their time than
to make fun of you."

Bruin doubted it, and when they drew near the patrol, he
saw the lieutenant in charge of the group burst out laughing
and then nudge the sergeant beside him. A moment later, the
entire mounted patrol was hee-hawing so uproariously that
they were nearly falling out of their saddles.

"Good afternoon!" the lieutenant shouted, wiping tears
from his eyes and then doffing his hat toward Ophelia. He

read the writing on the medicine shack and said, "Dr. Health, it is a supreme pleasure to meet you and your little helper."

"I'm *not* his little helper," Ophelia snapped, watching the men continue to hovel and point at the poorly drawn figures and the crude words scrawled across the wagon's sides extolling the virtues of the good doctor's special tonics, elixirs, and salves.

"Got any free samples?" the lieutenant asked.

"No, sir!" Bruin answered, slapping the backs of his odd team and urging them to pass around the laughing cavalry patrol.

"Hold on there!" the sergeant called, reaching out to grab the lines.

Maggot's yellow teeth clamped on the sergeant's arm, causing the man to holler with pain. This pleased Bruin and put an immediate stop to the laughter.

"Sir!" the lieutenant shouted in anger. "Your ugly white mule is a danger and a menace. He has probably broken my sergeant's arm!"

"If he has," Bruin replied, "it will be a good lesson in manners. Your man reached for my reins without permission. He got what was coming to him!"

"Sergeant?"

The man was in serious pain. He sort of slid off his horse and collapsed on the ground, writhing in abject pain. "Sergeant, is your arm broken?"

"Dunno!" he screamed, face twisted in agony.

"Corporal Denning," the lieutenant ordered. "Dismount and have a look at the sergeant's arm. If it's broken, I mean to charge Dr. Good Health with assault."

"I didn't do anything to him!" Bruin protested. "It was the mule that bit your man and you can't arrest a mule. Besides, your sergeant damn sure had it coming."

The lieutenant was in his mid-thirties, ferret-faced, with a hooked nose and close-set eyes. He ignored Bruin as his sergeant was given attention.

"I think his arm is just badly bruised," Corporal Denning

finally reported after struggling to roll up the man's sleeve. "I'd say it's bruised down to the bone. That white mule really chomped him hard."

The lieutenant swore under his breath, then glared at Bruin. "Well, Dr. Health," he said in a cold, uncompromising voice, "according to the advertisements written on that wagon, you're the world's greatest healer."

"I didn't write that rubbish!"

"I don't care who wrote that drivel. Get your medicine and help my sergeant or else I'll arrest you on the spot!"

Bruin was about to reach for the gun at his side, but Ophelia whispered, "There's several boxes of medicine back in the wagon."

"Most of the bottles have popped their corks or are broken."

"Some aren't. Get one and medicate that soldier up before you're arrested and I have to go hunt my father alone."

"What is she telling you?" the lieutenant demanded.

"She's telling me to do as you ordered, so I guess maybe I will."

"You had better, and do it quick, Dr. Good Health."

"I'm not Dr. Good Health!" Bruin stormed. "I heard that he was a quack that made half of Flagstaff sick to their stomachs. In order to pay for damages, he had to leave his wagon behind, and so my granddaughter and I bought it cheap because—"

"I don't care about any of that! Get my sergeant some pain relief!"

"Do it," Ophelia urged. "You can't fight the whole bunch of them. They're the United States Army."

"They're a bunch of nitwits," Bruin grumbled, opening the door behind them and falling back inside the wagon.

He crawled to a box of foul-smelling bottles and pulled one out that still was stoppered with a cork. He'd inspected the reeking bottles earlier, and guessed that they contained the finely minced parts of rodents along with turpentine, bad corn liquor, and liberal doses of creosote and chili peppers. Bruin had made the mistake of sticking his finger in a bottle and then touching it to his tongue. That had been a mistake because the witch's brew had burned like fire and tasted like sulfur.

"If the sergeant wants something to take his mind off Maggot's bite, this ought to do 'er," Bruin mused aloud as he climbed out the back door of the medicine wagon and went over to attend the suffering sergeant.

"Here you go," he said, uncorking a bottle of the vile liquid and then kneeling beside the sergeant, who was still screaming. "Quit screaming like a child and open your mouth!"

The sergeant did as ordered, and Bruin placed a steadying knee on his chest, pinning him solidly to the ground a moment before he shoved the bottle halfway down his gullet and poured liberally.

The effect on the cavalryman was nothing less than miraculous. He vaulted straight off the ground from his back and knocked Bruin aside. Before anyone could react, the sergeant ran amok, arms windmilling crazily and eyes rolling like dice in a jar. He ran straight into a pine tree, flopped onto his belly, and began to make a sound like a dying coyote, or one with its tail all on fire. Finally, the sergeant quivered from toe to heel and passed out.

"What the hell is in that medicine!" Corporal Denning cried as everyone else dismounted and rushed to the stricken man's side. "Have you just poisoned our poor sergeant?"

"I don't know," Bruin truthfully answered.

"Best get out of here fast," the corporal advised before hurrying over to the sergeant and taking his pulse.

"Giddy up!" Bruin shouted, leaping up into the driver's seat and administering a sharp crack of the heavy leather reins against his mismatched team.

Ophelia jumped back into the wagon and pushed open the back door. "Bruin, do you think that poor soldier just died of poisoning?"

"If he did, then we're in even more trouble than we were

before." Bruin whipped the team into a fast trot. Maggot hated to trot, much less gallop, but Bruin was in such a hurry to get away from the cavalry patrol that he did not care.

FIFTEEN

—◆◆◆—

THE EX-MARSHAL OF Prescott was saddle sore when he rode into Flagstaff because, like Ophelia, he was not accustomed to long, hard miles on the back of a horse. Furthermore, his pack mule had proved to be stubborn and unwilling to keep pace with his mount.

Wade Kilpatrick was badly out of sorts when he tied his animals up in front of the local marshal's office. He was unshaven, and appeared to have aged at least five years since leaving Prescott behind with its citizenry angry enough to have him sent to prison.

He pinned on his marshal's badge, knowing that the local constable could not possibly have learned about his being chased out of Prescott. "Marshal?" he asked, pushing into the Flagstaff officer's crowded little office. "My name is Wade Kilpatrick and I'm the marshal down in Prescott. Do you have a minute to talk?"

"Of course!" The man stood and offered his hand with a broad and easy smile. He was younger than Kilpatrick, better-looking by any woman's eye, and four inches taller. Wade Kilpatrick disliked him immediately, but hid his feelings well.

"My name is Michael Peterson. What brings you to Flagstaff?"

"I'm hunting a killer and an orphaned girl that helped him break out of my jail"

The tall man's eyebrows lifted. "And you think he's hiding out in my town?"

"Is or was. He's a giant with a bushy salt-and-pepper-colored beard and mustache. Wears old buckskin leather shirts matted with blood and grease, and gray flannel pants that have holes in both knees. His name is Bruin Henry, and he has a big, crooked nose that's probably been busted over and over in brawls and a lot of scars around his face. And he smells something awful."

Peterson had begun to nod his head. "I saw such a man and he really stood out."

"Yeah," Kilpatrick agreed. "Bruin Henry is impossible to miss. He's riding a huge, white Missouri mule."

"Yep! I did see him. Didn't see a girl with him, though."

"I expect she was running around doing something or other."

"And you say this girl helped the giant escape?"

"That's right."

"Why?" Peterson asked.

Kilpatrick saw no reason to explain that Ophelia was Bruin's granddaughter, or that her mother had just suffered an early and painful death. No sense in generating any sympathy. "Who knows what goes on in the mind of a girl like that?"

Marshal Peterson's expression was one of deep concern. "Do you think the old man is . . . well, violating her?"

"You know something? It wouldn't surprise me."

The marshal of Flagstaff paled and then shook his head. "I wish I'd have known about this earlier. If you thought they were passing this way, why in blazes didn't you send me a telegraph?"

"I thought the pair were traveling south toward Tucson.

They fooled me by turning north and then coming through this way."

"I have a daughter," Peterson confessed. "Sylvia is only four, but just the thought of some dirty old coot messing or even thinking about messing with her or any other child makes my blood run cold."

"Mine too," Kilpatrick said grimly. "Can you help me find them?"

Peterson jumped for his hat and shoved it down with authority. "If they're still in Flagstaff, you bet I will!"

"It shouldn't be hard to find out," Kilpatrick said, deciding this man was an overeager fool. "I figure we just need to visit your liveries. Bruin Henry sets a great store by his white mule, even though it's meaner than a rattlesnake."

"Let's go," the marshal of Flagstaff said. "There are only four liveries in town. It won't take long to visit them and see if we can arrest that old degenerate."

"If we spot Bruin Henry, I'd strongly advise that we shoot first and ask questions later . . . if he's still alive," Kilpatrick urged. "He knows me and he'll go for his gun at the drop of a hat. Why, he's such a low-down skunk that he'll use the little girl as a shield."

The marshal swore. "If there's anything I hate, it's a man that will take advantage of a child."

"Me too," Wade Kilpatrick said, feeling very pleased with himself. Bruin Henry was a dangerous man, and it wouldn't hurt to have some backup from this stupid and gullible Flagstaff marshal.

"HE'S GONE," THE third liveryman they visited said. "The big man and that girl left almost two days ago."

"Did they say where they were headed?" Kilpatrick demanded, furious that he would have to keep riding.

"Afraid not. Was that giant in buckskins a real outlaw?"

"Bruin Henry is a killer many times over," Kilpatrick answered. "I tracked him from Prescott and came across four men that Henry had murdered. He didn't even bother to bury them."

"The giant had a powerful mule with a real nasty disposition," the liveryman said. "Meanest critter I've ever seen, but he was strong enough to pull a freight wagon all by himself. Only they put him in harness with a palomino."

Kilpatrick had been about to hurry away, but this news stopped him in this tracks. "What did you say, mister?"

"I said they left in a wagon."

"Why would they do that?"

"Because the girl had saddle sores. She couldn't ride anymore, so she talked the old man into buying a medicine wagon I happened to have for sale. It was—"

Kilpatrick wasn't sure he'd heard correctly. "They bought a what?"

"A medicine wagon. Marshal Peterson, you remember that red, white, and blue medicine wagon that the town fathers allowed me to have in exchange for my big unpaid livery bill. I thought I'd never get rid of that rolling pile of lumber, but the girl insisted it was perfect for their traveling needs. Her grandfather had other ideas, though."

It was Marshal Peterson's turn to be caught off guard, and now he stared at the liveryman. "Did you say that Bruin Henry is the girl's *grandfather*?"

"That's right. I heard her call him that."

Peterson turned on Kilpatrick with a look of confusion on his handsome face. "Marshal Kilpatrick, didn't you know that?"

"Uhh, I guess I forgot."

Peterson was not pleased. "Well, dammit, it makes a big difference. Here I was thinking I might have to deputize a posse to go after a rank old degenerate, but now I learn that the giant was the girl's grandfather."

"He could still be taking advantage of her," Kilpatrick said, the words sounding lame even to himself.

"Yes, he could," Peterson agreed.

"The girl's mother died in Prescott of a cancer," the liveryman volunteered. "Her name is Ophelia and she told me that they were looking for her father."

"Whose father?"

The liveryman said, "The girl was looking for her *own* father?"

A light seemed to go on inside Peterson's head. "And was the father a United States marshal named Link Cochran?"

"Why, yes, Marshal, I believe she did say her father's name was Link."

In anger, Marshal Peterson grabbed Kilpatrick by the shirt and turned him full around. "Say now, what the hell is going on here! I saw that girl and I helped her get a message from Denver. Her father had been a federal marshal, but he'd resigned and gone off to a place called Pine River on the Mogollon Rim."

"How far?" Kilpatrick asked, ready to bolt and run for his horse.

"About a hundred miles south and a bit east."

Kilpatrick batted the man's hand away and started to leave. "If Bruin and Ophelia are riding in an old medicine wagon, I'll catch up with them soon enough."

Before Marshal Peterson could say anything more, Kilpatrick was running up the street toward his horse.

"What's going on?" the liveryman asked, scratching his head.

"I don't know," Peterson said, "but this whole thing seems kind of fishy. Marshal Kilpatrick is from Prescott and he says that the big man in the buckskin shirt broke out of his jail thanks to the help of the girl. But he failed to mention that Henry was her grandfather or that she came here looking for her father."

"They were an odd pair, that's for sure, but I liked them both," the liveryman said. "The old man, he didn't say one whole hell of a lot, but he sure loved his mule. You can tell a lot by how a man treats his animals, and that big man had a good heart."

"Kilpatrick says that he's killed plenty of men. Some down in Prescott and four more on the way up here to Flagstaff."

The liveryman shrugged his narrow shoulders. "Well, he was big and strong enough to do it, all right. But you know what I'd do if I was you, Marshal Peterson?"

"What?"

"I'd send a telegraph down to Prescott and find out what *really* happened."

Peterson's brow knitted with worry. "But who would I send a telegram to if their marshal is here?"

"Send it to the town mayor."

"Fine idea!" Peterson exclaimed, suddenly grinning. He slapped his leg and cried, "Now, why didn't I think of that!"

The liveryman just shuffled his scuffed boots in the dust. But he knew the answer to the question. Marshal Peterson was handsome, brave, and charming, but it was all too obvious that the poor man didn't even have enough brains to come in out of the rain.

After the marshal left, Kilpatrick returned to the livery on horseback dragging a small and resistant mule. "Mister, do you want to buy my pack mule and her saddle!"

The liveryman shook his head. "She's too small and appears not to have a willing temperament."

"If you don't buy her, then I may have to shoot her!"

"There's Indians hereabouts that like the taste of mule meat. I'll give you ten dollars for her."

"That's outrageous!" Kilpatrick swore. "Why, she's worth fifty and the packsaddle at least another ten dollars."

"Then keep 'em for yourself," the liveryman said. "For I will not own an unwilling mule, and the Yavapai Indians are tough to deal with in this part of Northern Arizona."

Kilpatrick swore at the liveryman, at his horse, and especially at his difficult jenny mule. Then turned up the street and hurried southeast toward a town called Pine River.

SIXTEEN

—m—

"THE DAMNED WHEEL is coming off!" Bruin shouted a moment before the medicine wagon lurched heavily to the right and then smashed down on its axle, throwing both passengers off a steep mountain road.

Ophelia rolled perhaps twenty feet and grabbed a bush, but Bruin wasn't so quick or fortunate. He went tumbling head over heels, and didn't stop until he struck a boulder down in a narrow, brush-choked canyon filled with a cold and swift-running stream.

"Bruin!"

There was no answer. Ophelia could hear Maggot hee-hawing with distress, but the first priority was to get to her grandfather before he drowned. For all she knew, he might already be dead.

"Grandfather! Are you all right!"

He didn't move, so Ophelia took a deep breath and sledded on gravel and sharp, rolling rocks until she reached the bottom. Given her galling saddle sores, the experience was extremely unpleasant. When she reached Bruin, she saw that his face was buried in mud and water.

Ophelia grabbed him by his long, shaggy hair and pulled his head up, and he wasn't breathing.

"Bruin!" she screamed, trying to shake him. "Grandfather, please wake up!"

He coughed and spluttered, then roused and stared up at her with obvious confusion. "What . . ."

"This water is freezing cold," she told him. "We have to get you back up to the medicine wagon."

But Bruin shook his head, trying to focus on the grade leading up to their busted medicine wagon. "I'm not up to a climb, little darlin'. Why don't you go cook us up something to eat and bring me some of Dr. Good Health's bottled poison."

"You want to drink that awful medicine?"

He nodded. "The way I'm feeling, I need something that will either cure me or kill me."

Ophelia studied the long, difficult climb up to the road.

"You can do it," he urged. "Just angle back and forth on the slope and try to keep to the most solid footing."

Her brow was furrowed and her lips were thin and drawn in a hard, white line. "But it's all shale and so steep."

"You *have* to do it," he said, blinking as he realized that the noise from up above was Maggot hee-hawing in distress. "Go on now and see to the animals! If they can walk, then hitch 'em and get them down here to my side."

"How?" Ophelia looked wildly all around.

"I don't know," he admitted, fighting off waves of dizziness and nausea. "But find a way."

Her eyes were wet, and it was cold down in the canyon's bottom. "Grandpa, are you hurt real bad?"

Bruin wiggled his toes, then turned both ankles and examined his arms. When he tried to lift the left one, he choked back a groan. "My damned upper arm has gone and popped out of its shoulder socket."

"What can we do about that?"

"It's happened before," Bruin replied. "For the present, it will have to be left alone."

He arched his back with a grimace and a grunt.

"Is your back broken!"

"Naw. Just beat up like the rest of me. Ophelia?"

"Yes?"

"You *can* make it to the top. Getting Maggot and that mare down here is going to be a whole lot tougher."

"But what if I get blocked on this stream? There could be a place where big rocks come close together and the stream is too swift to—"

Bruin's voice cut hers to silence. "Maggot can swim if you come to a place down below that's narrow and filled with water. He's also the surest-footed animal alive. Jump on his back and give him his head. He's smart and he'll know where I am."

"How . . ."

Bruin reached out and placed his hand on her arm. "If the animals are still able to move, then lead Maggot over to the edge and I'll holler up to him. He'll see me and understand."

She looked doubtful.

"A smart dog could figure out where its master is and that he's been hurt. Mules are a lot smarter than dogs, Ophelia. So let Maggot see me and then saddle him and the mare. Once that's done, lead them down into this canyon where you can and start up the stream. I'll expect you here before nightfall."

"Then what will we do?"

"I'll crawl onto a rock, mount Maggot, and you'll mount the mare, and we'll ride back up to the wagon and see if it can be fixed or not. If not, we'll leave it behind and ride on. That's why I insisted we keep our saddles, blankets, and bridles."

"All right," she said, thinking that he might as well have suggested that she and the animals fly to the moon.

Bruin's hand edged downward to see if his gun was still resting in its holster. He had slipped a leather thong over the hammer of the pistol, and it was still in place. "Ophelia, don't forget to bring me a few bottles of that black medicine and also my Winchester."

"I get it. In case Marshal Kilpatrick catches us down here."

"Now you're thinking," Bruin told her as he closed his eyes and tried to stop the noisy grinding wheel slowly turning his brain to mincemeat. He didn't want to say anything to alarm Ophelia, but he felt as if he'd busted a few ribs.

"I'll find a way to do this," she vowed, trying to convince herself more than Bruin.

"I know that. Now listen to me carefully because what I have to say is very important."

"I'm listening."

"Ophelia, if you should see that damned marshal from Prescott coming hard up our back trail, jump on the mare and ride for all you're worth. He wants me a whole lot worse than he wants you, so you'd have time enough to get out of his sight."

Without realizing it, Ophelia was shaking her head violently. "I'm not leaving you here to be tortured by that . . . sonofabitch!"

He blinked. "Ophelia! Watch your mouth!"

But she wasn't finished. "I know a lot worse words than that, Grandpa. I wasn't raised in a convent, you know."

"Git!"

Ophelia leaned over and did something that was totally unexpected. She kissed Bruin on the cheek. It was just a little peck, but it was the first kiss he'd gotten since the moment his wife had died so many long and lonely years ago.

OPHELIA TACKLED THE shale with a vengeance. Again and again she threw herself at the canyon's side, but never got more than ten steps before the footing broke loose and she either fell backward or slid down again.

What am I going to do? The road is so far up and I'm getting nowhere at this rate.

She was panting, and every pore of her body bled sweat. It

was so hot and so desolate. Ophelia realized that she could not climb in the same shale area that she and Bruin had rolled down. She had to find another way out or they were trapped.

Should she go up this canyon or down? She tried to quiet her mind enough to judge each direction, measuring the angle of slope up to the road. After long moments of indecision, Ophelia decided that she had to search for a way out of this mess by going downstream. But even that direction did not seem very promising because there were immense boulders and fallen trees of all sizes and shapes clogging the narrow canyon. And how could she hope to bring a mount down into this death trap?

Ophelia had no answer, but she knew that she had to start moving. "Good-bye, Grandpa."

He didn't answer, and that worried her all the more. She did not know much about Bruin Henry except his murderous past, but she did know that he was not one to show pain or fear. He was probably hurt far worse than he'd told her, and that meant that time was critical. Her grandfather was huge and tremendously strong, but he was old and had suffered many terrible wounds. Once, when he didn't know she was close and watching, Bruin had removed his buckskin shirt, and Ophelia had been appalled by all the fearful scars on his torso. Several of them had even looked to be the puckered flesh of long-healed bullet holes.

Ophelia moved downstream, constantly on the alert for rattlesnakes or places where she might slip and fall or else pin her foot in between two rocks and break her ankle. If she were bitten by a snake or suffered a broken foot or leg bone, she knew that both she and Bruin very might well be found dead by Marshal Kilpatrick.

Just the thought of the lawman made Ophelia quicken her step to the point of it being dangerous. She hurried along the bank of the rushing stream, jumping over rocks and trying to keep her balance. Twice, she accidentally fell into the water, which was so cold in contrast to the hot air that it took her breath away. Did the sides of this canyon seem to be gradually widening, or was that just her imagination?

Hour after hour passed, and there were times when she had to wade into deep, blue pools, and once she was forced to swim. The water was swift and, in places, white with foam. How on earth could either Maggot or the mare ever return this way to reach Bruin?

At least he won't die of thirst, Ophelia told herself, finding solace in her grim and sardonic humor.

She kept looking up at where the road would be, always half expecting to see Wade Kilpatrick with a rifle sighted on her heaving chest. Ophelia began to despair, wondering if she would ever find a place where she stood any chance of climbing out of the canyon.

Finally, when the shadows were long and an owl screeched in the hot, dry wind, Ophelia found a game trail that appeared to lead all the way up to the wagon road. Gasping and shivering, she ran the first fifty yards up the trail, and then doubled over sucking wind. Two full minutes passed before she could straighten and then continue the climb. The game trail was well used and it zigzagged constantly, but gained altitude at a surprising rate.

Ophelia collapsed on the road as the sun was touching the western edge of the canyon. With no time to waste and knowing that she was going to have to retrace her steps in darkness, she trotted down the road for nearly two miles before she reached the medicine wagon.

Indians!

Ophelia didn't know what to do. Sick with dread and almost paralyzed by fear, she momentarily considered leaping over the side of the road and tumbling back into the canyon, but knew that would be the end of both her and Bruin Henry. However, she preferred to die battered or drowned rather than to be scalped.

The four Indians were as still and silent as stones as she wiped the perspiration from her eyes and tried to calm her mind. Only then did she realize that this was a family composed of a father, mother, and twin girls about her own age.

The family stood beside the busted medicine wagon and watched her as if she were some wild, unnamed beast that had emerged from the depths of middle earth, the source of their ancient creation.

"Hello?" Ophelia raised her hand palm facing forward, as she had seen others do with Prescott's Indians, who did little mischief when they were in town. "Me friend."

They nodded quite formally. The family was dressed in buckskin shirts like Bruin's, except theirs were far cleaner and better fitting. The wife and girls had on heavy cloth skirts, wine-colored and wide at the bottom with pleats. The man wore faded denim pants, and they all wore scuffed leather lace-up boots and ropes wrapped around their narrow waists instead of belts. They carried large sacks made of leather, and Ophelia could see that they were filled with what appeared to be slender, curved branches.

The man carried a rifle, and Ophelia was sure it belonged to Bruin Henry. He stood closest to the palomino and the busted wagon wheel.

"My name is Ophelia Cochran," she called as she took a few tentative steps closer, knowing that she should not run or the man might shoot her like a fleeing animal. "My grandfather is Bruin Henry and he is at the bottom of the canyon and is hurt very badly. Can you help us?"

All four of them leaned close together and began a whispered conference that ended when the father turned to Ophelia and answered in very good English, "What do you want us to do?"

"Help me get my grandfather out of the canyon before he dies."

The man went over to the edge of the canyon and stared down at Bruin. He motioned for his wife and daughters to join him, and they all gazed intently into the gathering gloom.

"My grandfather is very big and heavy," Ophelia rushed, "and he told me to bring the horse and mule down to him, but

I am afraid that they would never make up it the river from the game trail I used to escape."

Ophelia had to swallow hard because voicing the impossibility of the predicament made it all seem so hopeless. "My grandfather might even have died by now, but I can't just leave him down there to be eaten by animals. He has killed men, but I think he has repented somewhat, and I know that he deserves better than to die alone down in that awful canyon."

The family turned and studied her, and Ophelia felt her heart begin to pound. Would the man simply raise the Winchester and put a bullet in her chest? She tried to read their expressions, and failed. They were not a handsome family. They were short, squatty people with wide, flat faces and eyes that revealed none of their feelings.

"We will help you," the woman said.

Ophelia's knees almost buckled with relief. She jumped forward and cried, "Oh, thank you! Now, we have to unhitch the mule and the mare and then lead them back down there. It'll be dark and the way is—"

"No," the man said in a low but firm voice. "If you try that you would fail. We have to get him out by ourselves."

She didn't understand. "But how!"

"We must pull him out. Drag him up to the top."

Ophelia found herself shaking her head. "You don't understand," she said, trying to keep her voice calm and level. "My grandfather is a *giant*. A really, really big and heavy man. And his left arm has popped completely out of his shoulder socket."

"There is no other way," the woman said, her face displaying a softness that Ophelia had overlooked. "And we must hurry."

"But . . ."

"Stay here," one of the girls said in a gentle voice. "Protect the animals and your things. That mule is in trouble and the mare is shaking with fear."

"But . . ."

Ophelia sputtered, then clamped her mouth shut. These were Indians and they knew more about deep canyons and rivers and snakes and everything in the wild than she would in her entire lifetime. What they didn't know was that the shale was so loose that it was impossible to cross, much less climb.

The family held another quick conference as the sun touched the Western rim and filled the canyon with a color not unlike golden honey. The parents untied their rope belts, and their daughters did likewise.

Ophelia thought she understood their misguided plan. "Those belts all tied together won't be long enough," she told them, aware that she was no longer their primary interest. "Not nearly long enough."

"Stay here and take care of the animals, then rest," the woman told her. Ophelia realized she was shaking with fatigue and could not have done otherwise. She was spent, used up completely.

"Yes, ma'am," she replied, wanting nothing more than to go inside and lie down on one of the tilted cots. "I do need to get the mule and the palomino unhitched and watered from the barrel lashed to the side of the wagon."

"Yes, do that," said the man a moment before he disappeared over the side followed by his women.

Ophelia wanted to cry out a warning, but it was already too late. She ran to the edge of the road, and gazed down in astonishment as the Indians glided down the canyon side as if they were riding boards on snow. They didn't sit down and sled like Ophelia, and yet somehow, they maintained their balance all the way to the bottom. She saw them emerge from a cloud of dust and hurry to Bruin's side.

"I don't believe it," Ophelia said, hearing Maggot hee-hawing with growing impatience. "How did they do that!"

She squinted hard in the dying light, but couldn't see what was going on far down below. Suddenly, Bruin screamed and Ophelia's hands flew to her mouth in horror. *Oh, dear Lord, had she badly misjudged the Indians' moral intentions? Had*

*the father just drawn his knife and lifted Bruin's scalp! Oh, my
God, if he has . . .*

It was simply too awful to think about, so Ophelia staggered backward a few steps, then whirled and ran to the aid of
their distressed team. She decided right then and there that if
Bruin had just been scalped, she would jump on the mare and
ride for her life.

SEVENTEEN

—◦—

BRUIN HENRY HAD awakened with a scream in his ears. He opened his eyes and saw figures moving, then reached for his gun, but a gentle hand gripped his wrist and a voice said, "We had to pull your arm back in place so we can pull you up the side of this canyon. Better to do that before you awake. Don't hurt so bad maybe."

"It hurt some, but who are *you*?" He could see the moving figures and squinted hard, but it was too dark to make out faces.

"We are Apache. We are friends, and will help you out of this bad place."

" Apache?"

"Mogollones," the man said, then hastily added, "No relation to Geronimo."

Bruin studied them closer, and saw that they were a family. "You're not fixin' to scalp me?"

"No."

Bruin was a suspicious man when it came to the Apache,

and his hand moved down toward his holstered gun. "Why not?"

"Because we are Christian converts and Jesus tells us to help the poor and those in trouble."

"What about Ophelia?"

"The girl?"

"Yeah." Bruin sat up and gasped at the pain in his side, suddenly worried about his granddaughter. "I have to find her! Last time I saw Ophelia, she was heading downstream trying to get back up to Maggot and the mare."

"They are all well," the woman said in a soft voice. "Do you still have much pain?"

There was no paint in denying it. "Yeah, but I can handle a few busted ribs and whatever else is wrong." He lifted his right arm. It hurt something fierce at the point of his shoulder, but that was expected, and he knew it would be very sore for the next week. "What are we going to do now?"

"Climb out," the Apache said, pointing up the impossibly steep scree.

"We'll never make it. At least I won't. Bruin squinted hard. "Are those your daughters?"

"Yes."

"You shouldn't have brought them or your woman down into this canyon. We may never get out."

The Apache and his wife spoke in their native tongue for several minutes. It was a fast, guttural sound, and one that Bruin could make neither heads nor tails of. They both started tracing an escape route with their fingers, and Bruin couldn't help saying, "It's no use, I tell you."

But the Apache thought different. The parents ordered their daughters to attack the slope. Bruin watched the girls fight for each foot of ground, often sliding back, only to try again. He was about to tell them that they were wasting their time and energy, when one of the girls seemed to get her footing. She called out and the other daughter followed. The lead one grabbed a sharp stick and began to poke furiously at the gravel, and soon they seemed to have discovered some harder ground covered only by several inches of gravel.

"Can you stand and walk?" the Apache man asked Bruin.

"I can try."

They helped him to his feet, and Bruin shook himself all over and refused to look up the slope because it seemed such a waste of time for him to even attempt the climb. On the other hand, the girls were making progress as they poked at the gravel and worked their way higher and higher.

The woman also found a poking stick and said, "Can you come with us now?"

"Sure," Bruin gritted, allowing them to step in close on each side and hold him by the arms as if he were a doddering old invalid.

It took Bruin and the Apache nearly two hours to climb out of the canyon, and they fell so many times that they lost count. They finally topped the road, and Bruin collapsed with the sound of Ophelia shouting with jubilation.

"You did it!" she kept repeating. "You *all* did it!"

Bruin raised himself up on his elbows. He was battered and laced with cuts and rock dust. His thick legs were trembling and sweat stung his eyes as they crinkled at the corners, and he watched his granddaughter and the Apache girls grab hands and do a little celebration dance.

When it was over, Bruin let them help him back to his feet and then wipe the dust and sweat from his face with a rag wetted in the rain barrel. He made his way over to Maggot, who had been unhitched hours ago and was now tied to the canted three-wheeled wagon. Both the mule and the mare were wearing feed bags, which told Bruin they had been grained.

"How you doin', old fella," he said, reaching up and scratching the big animal behind its long ears. "Did you think you'd seen the last of me this time? Well, if you did, then I can admit that so did I."

He removed Maggot's empty feed bag and found some more grain for the beast. Maggot's ears came forward and he was happy.

There was enough moonlight for Bruin to inspect the errant wagon wheel and determine that all the spokes were intact and the hub was still solid. Ophelia and the Apache watched him, and Bruin solemnly announced, "It'll do if we can get it back on the axle."

"We can lift the wagon," Ophelia said. "Then you can wrestle it back on and fix it so it won't come off again."

"I can make it do for a while," Bruin said. "But what it needs is the services of a wheelwright, or at least a good blacksmith."

The Apache girls, whose names were Nana and Camila, both told her that there was a little settlement about twenty miles to the south, but that it was a bad place filled with evil people who robbed innocent travelers.

"Our father will go there alone to sell our antlers," Nana said, pointing to the large burlap sacks that Ophelia had thought contained wood. "We don't go into that place, but instead hide in the trees and wait until he is finished selling."

"You sell antlers?"

"Yes. But first we make many of them into very useful things," Camila told her. "Mostly knife handles that Father shapes and polishes."

"And that is how you make your money?"

"We also work when we can find it," the father said. "My name is Johnny and my wife is named Judith. We were captured by the whites when we were small and raised by missionary priests. We were taught to read and write, but that hasn't done us any good."

"Some good," Judith corrected. "We read the Holy Bible and sometimes a newspaper."

"But we are always traveling. Hunting for work or antlers of the deer and elk to make things to sell."

Bruin took this all in, and was amazed. "You people are welcome to come along with us for as long as you like. We'd have been cooked without your help. There's food in the wagon, which reminds me that I'm starving. We also have medicine in bottles that tastes like pig piss, but will make us all happy enough to dance."

"No!" Ophelia said. "Bruin, you're not going to pollute this fine Christian family!"

"Going to what?"

"*Pollute*. Contaminate their bodies."

Bruin didn't know what to say about the Apaches' bodies, but his was in so much hurt that he reckoned it could stand a fair amount of pollution. "Let's cook a meal right here and have a feast. Ophelia, you and the girls gather some firewood and then set to work cutting up some pork for bacon. I'll get the pollution."

He tried to raise his leg and climb into the wagon but his ribs and limbs just wouldn't cooperate. "Ophelia, I sure could use your help for a minute."

"I will not be a party to your debauchery."

"You sure got a way with words," Bruin said proudly. He gritted his teeth and hauled himself up into the wagon, where he found a bottle. He knew the first few swallows were going to be awful, but he had drunk about everything there was short of pure poison and knew that, if there was enough alcohol in Dr. Good Health's medicine, then he would soon feel much, much better.

"Grandpa! You are the worst!" Ophelia stormed with exasperation.

He upended the bottle and swallowed fast, expecting the worst, and was not in the least bit disappointed. Bruin let out a hoarse holler and emptied the bottle. He would drink one more, and then he would try to lift the damned wheel and get it fixed on the hub. A second bottle, a good sizzling bait of bacon, fried potatoes, and beans, he'd be ready for the road.

"Johnny," he said and a few minutes later when the man helped him down from the wagon. "As soon as we eat and get the wheel fixed, we need to move along quick."

"You need rest. Travel again tomorrow morning."

"Well," Bruin said, taking a long, shuddering swig of the witch's brew, "that would normally make the most sense. But

I need to tell you that we are being followed by a lawman determined to shoot both Ophelia and myself dead."

They had a campfire and the bacon was frying. Johnny looked up, the firelight reflecting his surprise and concern. "What have you done?"

"It's a long story, but the short of it is that we shamed the marshal of Prescott when Ophelia and Maggot busted me out of his jail cell. Then, my granddaughter tricked him with fool's gold instead of the real thing. What it all amounts up to is that, if the marshal should happen to catch us, he might be so crazed that he'd shoot you and your whole family plumb dead."

"Why?"

"He's a bad man," Ophelia explained. "His gods are greed and gold."

The Apache nodded. "There are very many such bad men."

"What grandfather is saying is that it isn't safe to be with us. Maybe you and your family should just go on ahead."

Johnny and Judith had another conference in their own tongue. The girls listened, then offered a few words. When the conference ended, Johnny said, "We will travel with you to the town."

"Is it Pine River?" Ophelia asked expectantly.

"No. Pine River is the *next* town."

"That's where I hope to find my father. He'll sure protect us from that damn . . . I mean, darn Marshal Wade Kilpatrick!"

Bruin said nothing, but instead took another pull on the bottle, then grunted, "Johnny, let's all of us get that wagon wheel on while I'm still upright, moving, and half sober."

The Apache could smell the vile brew, and well knew what the huge old man was drinking and that it would do neither him nor his spirit good. But he also knew from experience that you could not tell a man what to do because that usually made him all the more determined to do the thing that was so bad for him.

*   *   *

IT TOOK LESS time to get the wheel in place and their odd team back in harness than it did to feast by the fire on the lonesome mountain road flanked by tall, stately ponderosa pines. In the silence of the night, Bruin could hear the stream gurgle far down in the canyon, and he still could not believe that he and Ophelia were alive and ready to roll.

He raised his bottle of Dr. Health's brew in a sloppy toast and said, "To the good Apaches!"

Johnny managed a thin smile. "And to the good, sober, and godly whites when they can be found."

Bruin didn't know about the man's toast. Had his mind been clear and his body not wracked with pain, he would have given the words some serious thought. But given the circumstances, he decided to hell with it. These were fine Christian people and if there was a God, then he deserved thanks for sending them along to help at just the right place and time.

EIGHTEEN

—◆—

A ROOSTER WAS crowing and the sun was lifting off the mountains when the medicine wagon bumped into a run down and nameless settlement consisting of one house, a saloon, and a few boarded-up buildings. Dr. Health's elixir had about worn off, and Bruin was again feeling none too chipper. "Ophelia, I doubt we'll find a either a livery or a blacksmith in such a poor place."

But Ophelia raised her arm and pointed. "I see a barn at the far end of the street."

Bruin saw it now, but the blacksmith and livery, like the settlement itself, appeared almost abandoned. There were only two horses in the corrals, and the barn door was closed. He saw a few wagons in various states of repair, and guessed that the blacksmith had either died or left for lack of business.

"Whoa," he said to the team when they stopped in front of the ramshackle barn. He was still wondering why he saw no people astir. He turned around to look for the Apache, but the Indians were nowhere in sight. "Ophelia, did you see which way John and his family went?"

"No, and it's sure strange that they didn't at least tell us good-bye."

"Yeah, it is."

Bruin remained on his wagon seat, his head turning back and forth as he sized things up and found them not to his liking. He remembered the Apache saying that this was a bad place, and now wished he'd asked them why it was bad. To his way of thinking, this was like a ghost town. Still, he did note that there several corralled horses at the livery, as well as a handsome red rooster and several hens scratching out their breakfast as if everything were right and normal.

"What do you make of this, Grandpa? It's so quiet."

"I don't like the feel of it. It's like a ghost town." Bruin cupped his hands to his mouth and shouted. "Is anybody here?"

He heard coughing from within the barn. "Did you hear that?"

"I sure did. Someone is in that barn." Ophelia shivered in the still morning's coolness. "Maybe we ought to just keep going until we reach Pine River. There's something about this place that gives me the creeps."

"I have the same feeling, but Maggot and your mare need grain and water. And don't forget that our wagon wheel needs attention; there's no telling how much longer it will stay on that hub. If it falls off again, it could splinter the axle and then we'd be in a real pickle."

"I still say we should keep moving," Ophelia argued. "The Apache said this was a place where evil lived."

"We'll see if we can get our animals taken care of and the wagon wheel firmed," Bruin insisted. "We can't afford to break down on the road again, so you just sit still while I find out where everyone has gone."

He had to bite his lip to keep from grunting with pain as he slowly climbed down. Bruin banged hard on the barn's sagging front door. "Anyone around to help fix a wagon wheel!"

Hearing a weak reply, Bruin opened the door, ignoring the

tortured squeal of rusty hinges, and then he peered inside. "Mister, I couldn't hear you too well."

"Help!"

He drew his gun and stepped inside quickly, then waited a few moments for his eyes to adjust to the darkness. A huge barn owl shifted somewhere up in the dusty rafters, then decided to leave through a large crack in the wall. Bruin hardly noticed. "Mister, where are you?"

"Over here!"

"You been shot?"

"No."

"Then what's wrong with you!" Bruin demanded. "Answer up because I'm not in the mood to be trifled with this morning."

"I got the fever. Everyone here is fevered or already dead."

Bruin felt the hair on the nape of his neck stand up and prickle. "You got the yellow or the typhoid fever?"

"I got the killin' fever!"

"Maybe I'll just leave."

"No, please! I'm so thirsty. Water. All I ask is water."

"Why don't you get it yourself?"

"Too weak," the man whispered. "Too sick with the fever."

"How'd you and this town come to such a sad end?" Bruin asked, torn between giving the man a drink from a water barrel nearby or getting out of this place in one hell of a big hurry.

The man coughed and groaned. When he answered, his voice was weak and scratchy. "Sick folks passed through here last week and when they left, we all started coming down with chills, fever, and cramps."

"I'm no doctor, nor am I a minister, so I can't help you."

The man made a sobbing sound. "I just don't want to die of thirst. I'm on fire! Could you just bring me a bucket of water?"

Bruin found himself backing up fast. He retreated out of the door and stood in the sunshine feeling icy sweat bead on his forehead.

"What's wrong?" Ophelia asked.

"This place has fever. Everyone is either dead or dying. Man inside wants water."

"Then give it to him."

Bruin wasn't listening. "Ophelia, drive the team through town and then wait for me."

She was halfway out of her seat. "Bruin, what on earth are you talking about?"

He looked up at her. "I'll see what can be done here and then catch up with you."

"No!" Ophelia jumped down from the medicine wagon and planted her feet in the dust. "I'm not skipping out and leaving you or a bunch of sick people behind."

"Child," he said, "don't you be forgetting what John said about this place. It's evil and they rob people that pass through, and probably kill them to keep them silent. Besides, I doubt that there is anyone left alive except that fella inside the barn."

"We have to be sure."

"Dammit, Ophelia, you don't understand! Get back on that wagon and drive on out of town now!"

"I couldn't live with myself if there is someone in one of these houses in need of attention."

Bruin wasn't afraid of death, but Ophelia was so young. "There's nothing you could do here."

"I could give them water and prayers."

Bruin swore in helpless fury. "Listen," he said, almost pleading, "I'm a tough old man who has lived through fevers and pestilence. But you're young and with your whole life yet to live. So just . . ."

But before he could say another word, Ophelia turned and ran for the nearest house.

Bruin knew chasing her would be useless because he couldn't begin to run as fast as Ophelia. So rather than watch her go inside one of the houses filled with deadly sickness, he found a water bucket and filled it from a mossy trough outside. He groped his way through the barn to a little room where a thin and dying man lay on a bed beside a table with a flickering candle almost burned to its puddle base.

"Who are you?" the man gasped.

"Like I said, I'm no healer with the power of the Lord, and I'm no doctor, so it just don't matter."

"No," the man said, "I guess it don't. Lay the water bucket down here beside my bed and get the hell out of here. No sense in you getting sick and dying."

Bruin tried to guess the man's age, but failed. He just looked drawn and near death. "How long have you been sick?"

"Four or five days. We all came down with the fever in a hurry. I'm the last of the family."

"Everyone here was related?"

"The men were. The women were just whores that never said where they came from or where they wanted to go next." The man used the dipper in the pail to pour water over his face. He wasted more than he swallowed as he studied Bruin in the candle's faint light. "The light is almost gone. Third candle I've used and it's the last one."

"I could find you another, I guess."

"No," he said. "When it's finished . . . I'm finished. Say, you're a big one, ain't you."

"I'm big," Bruin agreed, taking a few steps back. "How many you reckon died of the fever?"

"There were three women and eight of us men. We should have killed that family slow that gave us the sickness."

"You killed a lot of folks passing through?"

He nodded. "We did. Spent all the money we stole on them whores and on liquor. Had us some fun, you can be sure."

"You wouldn't have been able to kill me," Bruin said. "Not without some of you dying first."

"Easy to say," the man told him. "We were good. Just looked like regular folks until we got the drop on you, then it was too late and you'd be dead. Didn't kill and rob everyone, though. Just did it when we needed the money or were bored."

"I think you got what was coming," Bruin told the man. "Maybe I'll leave you now to think about what you did and where you're about to go."

He cackled. "You mean to hell?"

"I didn't say it, but I guess that's right."

"Mister, we're all going to hell. Don't you know we are all sinners?"

"I guess that's true enough," Bruin said, "but some are a damn sight worse than others."

He had heard enough, and was turning to leave when the man cried, "Wait!"

"What for?"

"I don't want to die like this."

"I can't help you."

"Yes, you can," the dying man insisted. "Give me your gun."

"Not too damn likely."

"I got *money* hidden. Money enough to buy you ten guns."

Bruin sensed a trick, but the man's voice was so desperate he wasn't sure. "Where is it?"

"Your gun and then I'll tell you. I've got money hidden right here in this room."

Bruin shook his head. "You want to take one more man with you to hell and it ain't going to be me."

"All right. The money is hidden under that floorboard in a metal box."

"Which floorboard?"

"Third one from the wall. The one with no nails holding it down."

"Is it blood money?"

"It's just money! Take it and give me your gun."

Bruin went over and pulled up the board. Sure enough, there was a metal box, and when he opened it, a wad of green-backs.

"That's over a hundred dollars. Keep it but give me your damn gun. I don't want to die here alone. This barn is crawling with rats."

"Are you sure?"

"Yes!"

Bruin unholstered his weapon.

"Just throw it over here, then leave and burn every stick in this settlement right to the ground."

"What?"

"You heard me right. Put a match to every building. Fever can hang around after it kills, you know."

"I know, but what's a man like you care if someone else comes along and gets sick and dies? You already admitted that everyone here was no damn good."

"Yeah, but . . . well, why shouldn't even a man like me do one good thing before he dies? Just in case there is a God, huh?"

"I guess you can."

"Say, what's your name?"

"Bruin Henry. I'm traveling with my granddaughter, Miss Ophelia Cochran."

"Your granddaughter?" he asked with a smirk. "That's a good one!"

Bruin stepped back into the shadows. This man was evil, and he didn't have a right to die easy, but neither could Bruin leave him to be eaten by rats when he might still be conscious. So Bruin stuffed the cash into his pocket and pitched the dying man his gun a moment before he stepped into the shadows where he would not be a target.

"See you in hell, Bruin Henry!"

"Yeah."

Bruin hurried outside, and he had not even reached the medicine wagon when he heard the gunshot. He found a match and a handful of grass hay, then made a torch. Maggot's eyes rolled in fear for the mule was afraid of nothing except a fire. Bruin ignored his mule and took a few steps back inside the livery before he set the place to flame.

Smoke was pouring out the big livery door when he drove the team back through town, found Ophelia, and climbed down. She was sitting on a log, her head hanging low and resting on her hands.

"Bruin, they're all dead."

"We have to leave here just as soon as I torch the other buildings."

She raised her head. "You're going to burn everything?"

"Yes," Bruin explained, "because a killing fever lives on and on."

With the taste of smoke in the air, Bruin looked to the north where Marshal Kilpatrick would be coming to kill them both. "Ophelia, time is passing."

"All right. What do you think happened to Johnny, Judith, and their daughters Nanna and Camila?"

"I think they got scared before they got to this place."

"Will we see them again?"

"I don't know," Bruin answered. "Maybe."

"I hope so."

"So do I."

THEY FIRED THE buildings, then hurried to their medicine wagon to discover the Mogollon Apache family waiting in grim silence. Bruin and John studied each other for a moment, then watched the rising flames.

"We have to go now," Bruin said.

"Everyone here was cursed," the Apache proclaimed as the roof of the barn caved in sending up a tower of embers.

"That wasn't a very Christian thing to say," Ophelia told him with a hint of reprimand in her voice because she was still unaware of the evilness of the settlement and its people.

The Indian blinked at the rebuke, then explained, "We are Apache and Christian. Not one or the other alone. And I knew those and think they all will go to hell."

"I think you're probably right," Bruin said. "Now let's push on and see how far that bad wheel will carry us along before we have to leave this medicine wagon behind."

Ophelia was more than ready to leave. "I will tell my fa-

ther about this place," she said. "I doubt he knows about it or
he'd have arrested the whole bunch."

Bruin had to bite his lip to keep from telling Ophelia just
how ridiculous her words sounded. From what he remembered of Link Cochran, the man would have been right at
home among this den of whores, murderers, and thieves.

NINETEEN

—✺—

SOMEHOW, THE FAULTY wagon wheel stayed on all the way to Pine River, although it had begun to wobble the last few miles. The town of Pine River was larger than either Bruin or Ophelia had expected. It wasn't as big as Flagstaff or Prescott, but they'd already driven past two busy lumber mills, and there were some good-sized cattle ranches in the area. Bruin had asked a man walking along the road if there was any mining in these parts. He'd said there were copper mines about twenty miles to the south, but not much in the way of gold or silver.

"This is a nice big town," Ophelia said as they passed a church and a schoolhouse. "I can see why my father would want to come here."

"Don't be too disappointed if he's already left," Bruin said to her. "And anyway, our first stop is at the blacksmith shop."

John, Judith, and their girls had been riding in the medicine wagon and now the Apache family jumped out into the street. "We have things to sell," John said, trotting up to the front of the wagon with a bag of antlers slung over his broad shoulder.

"Good luck," Bruin called.

"Same to you and Ophelia. Maybe we'll see you again before we leave this town."

"I hope so," Bruin answered, meaning it. He had been considering the possibility of asking these good Apache people if they might be interested in helping him mine his gold. Sure, they didn't know anything about that kind of business, but they were hard working and he trusted them more than some white men that he might try to hire in a saloon. But it all depended on what happened when they found Link, so Bruin kept his silence as he watched the family head for the nearest general store.

"I doubt they make much money selling antlers," Ophelia said. "Their clothes are in poor shape."

"I noticed. Maybe they'll find steady work and prosper here. Looks like lots of folks are keeping themselves busy."

"Nana said that the white bosses at the lumber mills won't give their father work because they are Apache."

"A lot of folks hold hard feelings toward the Apache for the trouble they've caused."

"And we've caused *them*. The Indians were here first. Nana and Camila were telling me about all the trouble they have because of being Indians. The fact that they can read and write better than a lot of white people and are Christians doesn't mean anything to people with closed minds."

"I expect it doesn't," Bruin replied.

"There's the marshal's office!" Ophelia shouted, jumping from the wagon into the street. "Maybe my father is sitting inside right now!"

Bruin just grunted, knowing that there was no use in trying to slow Ophelia down. Her excitement over the possibility of seeing her father had been growing until the girl was ready to burst.

If he's actually there, Bruin reasoned, *maybe he won't try to kill me on sight. Perhaps the sight of his daughter will make him have a change of heart. And although I've sworn to kill him, I couldn't just shoot him down with Ophelia watch-*

*ing. Even if I did manage to kill Link, I'd lose whatever love
or respect I've earned from that girl.*

Bruin's heart was pounding as he drove over to the black-smith's shop and he checked his weapons. He didn't want to kill Ophelia's father and turn the girl against him, but he wasn't about to roll over and let himself be shot. Link was fast and accurate with a gun, and Bruin knew that he could not match the man in a stand-up fight.

"Hello there!" Bruin called to the blacksmith, who was a big fellow, nearly as large as Bruin and twenty or thirty years younger.

"Looks like you got problems."

"Yeah," Bruin said, reining the team up under a pine tree and climbing down from the wagon. "We're lucky to be here."

"That wheel needs work, all right."

"How long will it take and how much will it cost?" Bruin asked the brawny fellow.

"Cost you ten dollars and it'll take two days because I have a couple of jobs ahead of you from locals."

Bruin scratched his beard, keeping one eye on the blacksmith and the other on the marshal's office, where Ophelia had gone inside. "Well, mister, your price is fair, but I'd like to move along sooner. How about twenty dollars and you have it ready for me by five o'clock this afternoon?"

The blacksmith grinned. "For twenty dollars, I could do that."

"Figured so," Bruin answered.

The blacksmith stared at the wagon, lips moving slowly as he read the advertising. Finally, he turned to Bruin. "Are *you* Dr. Good Health?"

"Hell, no."

"That's a relief."

"Why?"

"Because you don't look to be in that much good health."

Bruin was offended, and had it not been for his ribs and the very real possibility that he was about to face Link in a gunfight, he might have challenged this disrespectful pup. "If you live as long and as well as I have," he growled, "you'll be a lucky man."

"I expect you're right," the blacksmith replied, his attention now on Maggot. "That sure is one fine mule."

"He's a good one, all right."

"I'll bet he weighs about fifteen hundred pounds."

"More like eighteen hundred," Bruin said, grabbing his rifle from the wagon and checking it over carefully.

The blacksmith clucked his tongue with admiration and walked all around Maggot, who snapped his teeth in warning. "He's spirited, ain't he?" the man said.

"You could call him that. I'd just call him ornery. Don't you get too close or he'll take a chomp out of you the size of an apple."

"Oh, I'll keep out of his range," the man said. "Why, I'll bet he can pull a big pine tree right out of the ground, roots and all."

"Probably so," Bruin said, "but Maggot doesn't like to pull. He prefers to be ridden."

"Is he fast?"

"Only when he has to be."

"Are you interested in selling him?"

"Nope." Bruin studied the marshal's office. "Is Marshal Link Cochran in town?"

"He left here about two days ago."

Bruin didn't know if he was glad to hear this news or not. He'd been waiting to have his showdown with Link for so many years that it was hard to know exactly what he felt anymore. All he knew for sure was that he'd live another day and that Ophelia would be very disappointed that her father had left Pine River. He saw her emerge from the office, shoulders slumped with disappointment.

"I'll be back at five o'clock," he said, turning to meet her.

"He's gone," Ophelia said, trying to keep from crying.

"Will he be back?"

"He's supposed to be. The bank was robbed two days ago.

My father and two men he deputized rode out to capture them and return the bank's money. They were expected back sooner. Everyone is waiting and plenty worried. If the bank money isn't recovered, a lot of people in this town will go under."

"Who told you all that?"

"The man in the marshal's office. He's a nice fella named Shorty. He says he's just sitting in until my father returns with the bank's money and his new prisoners."

Bruin took this all in without a word or any expression that would reveal his thinking. He didn't want to tell Ophelia that, unless he was badly mistaken, Link Cochran would *never* return and neither would the bank's money. Most likely, Ophelia's father had been in on the bank holdup and then had pretended to go chasing after his own friends. Bruin guessed that Link and the bank robbers had divided up the loot and were long gone by now.

"How much money did the bank robbers get?" Bruin asked.

"I didn't ask. It's not important." Ophelia looked up at him, tears at last filling her eyes. In an angry voice she cried, "Bruin, don't you get it? My father is chasing a bunch of desperate bank robbers who will try to kill him! Maybe they already have."

Too late Bruin realized his mistake, and said, "Now, don't get all upset, Ophelia. I have a hunch that your father is still alive."

She sniffled, but looked hopeful. "Bruin, do you really think so?"

"I'd be willing to bet on it."

"I hope you're right. Can we go after them?"

"Your father and those bank robbers?"

"Sure! Who else? Maybe my father needs our help."

Bruin pursed his lips as if engaged in deep and serious contemplation. "Well, Ophelia, I suppose we could. But we'd have to leave the medicine wagon behind. Wheel won't be fixed until late this afternoon."

"We could saddle up the mare and Maggot and ride."

"The animals need graining and rest. They're plumb tuckered out and so are we. I'm getting old, you know, and my ribs are giving me some grief. I think it would be best if we waited at least until tomorrow before we jump the gun."

"But there were four bank robbers, which means that my father and his two deputies are outnumbered."

"I still think we ought to give it until tomorrow."

"I don't!"

"Ophelia," Bruin said trying to sound reasonable, "we need to be calm about this. Your father is a good man with a gun and he knows how to take care of himself."

"But what if they ambush him?"

"He'll be watching for that and won't let it happen."

"But you can't know that for sure."

"No," Bruin admitted, "I can't. But we are staying here until tomorrow. If your father and his deputies haven't returned by then, we'll take up his trail."

It was abundantly clear from her expression that Ophelia didn't agree, but she nodded and said, "I'll get my bag and then find my own boardinghouse for the night."

"You could use a bath and some cleaning up," Bruin told her.

"So could you!" she yelled, stomping away as mad as a wet hen.

Bruin glanced down at his leather shirt, and realized how dirty and torn it was after his long tumble and hard climb out of the canyon. He reached into his pockets and found the hundred dollars that he'd gotten from the dying liveryman. Maybe he'd buy himself a new leather shirt and pants if any could be found to fit him in Pine River.

He ran his forgers through his long, tangled hair, picking at sticks and grit. He'd get a bath first, though, and maybe a haircut, but not a clean shave. Just trim up his mustache and beard a bit. Hell, if he was going to be shot down by Ophelia's father, he might as well leave this world looking respectable for his funeral service.

He found a hotel, then the barber and the bath, and finally he went to the town's largest general store. They stocked a red woolen shirt that he could squeeze into, and stiff blue bib overalls with straps over the shoulders. Farmer's pants, Bruin disdainfully called them.

"I was hoping for a leather shirt, one like this," Bruin told the proprietor as he held the tattered and bloodstained shirt up for their mutual inspection.

"You better take that thing out in the alley and burn it. The only way you'll find a leather shirt is to locate some Indian woman to tan a deer hide and sew it up to your size," the clerk reasoned. "Nobody wears leather outfits like that anymore. You old-time mountain men have all but disappeared. Hell, that's the kind of thing that Davy Crockett would have worn at the Alamo!"

"I'm not *that* damn old, and I've had plenty of friends that prefer leather to wool shirts."

"No offense, mister. There's an Apache reservation about fifty or sixty miles to the south of us, and you could probably have one sewn for you there."

Bruin held up the farmer's pants and the red wool shirt, and decided to hell with it. He would keep wearing what he had, and maybe Johnny and Judith would know of someone who still made good leather shirts, and even could fit him with a pair of leather pants. They were hot to wear in Arizona's low desert country, but it didn't hurt a man to sweat, and they wore like iron if you kept them greasy with fresh animal fat.

"Guess I'll just take a couple of those new handkerchiefs, some socks and a pair of boots . . . if you got any that fit."

The man glanced down at Bruin's feet. "Nope. You got feet darn near as big as webbed snowshoes. There's a cobbler and boot maker just five doors up the street." He chuckled. "You know what?"

"No, what?"

"Why, mister, I'll bet our boot maker could butcher a couple of large steers and make you a brand-new pair."

"Very funny," Bruin said, his eyes sparking with indignation so plain that the clerk gulped and lost his idiotic grin.

Bruin had already lost patience with town people. He would see a barber and then visit a saloon before eating and sleeping. But he'd not get into any trouble this night.

No, sir. He had enough trouble already with Ophelia mad at him and Link out there somewhere still robbing, cheating, and killing good folks.

TWENTY

—◦—

BRUIN WAS SHORN, bathed, and filled with a good breakfast when he went to visit Pine River's highly touted boot maker. Actually, he didn't expect to find a pair of ready-made boots, and he wasn't disappointed.

"I could measure you up a pair," the smallish man with the round eyeglasses said. "I could have them for you in two weeks and they'd cost . . . oh, twenty dollars given that I'd have to use extra shoe leather."

"Naw," Bruin said. "I won't be around in two weeks."

"Where will you be?"

"Most likely I'll either be planted in your local cemetery or over by the Superstition Mountains. Either way, I won't be needing your new boots."

"Why would you be dead?" the man asked, looking genuinely puzzled. "You're a bit long in the tooth, but you look fit as a fiddle."

"Thank you, but it's a personal matter."

"Death usually is," the man said. "The way I see it, we have no choice where we are born or under what circumstances. We often go through life trapped in some job or profession that we were pushed into by circumstances we don't even recognize. We meet very few interesting or intellectual people, and then we marry and have children never really having any choice in their being boys or girls or good or bad. We either are sickly or healthy depending on circumstances usually beyond our understanding or control, and then we come to the point of death. Finally, if we are fortunate and do not die suddenly, we can choose how we exit this cruel and indifferent world."

Bruin nodded without a clue of what the man was saying. "Sounds about right, mister, but you've lost me a bit on all that circumstances business."

The boot maker cleared his throat and frowned with concentration. "Well, think of it this way. What if you were born in, say, China or Africa instead of the United States? Do you think you'd act and look different than you do now?"

"I expect I would."

"Of course you would! And what if your parents had been pygmies in Africa? Do you think you'd be as huge a man as you are now?"

"Most likely not. Small people generally have small kids and big people big kids."

"Of course! What I'm saying is that we are what we are because of circumstances, and the only thing we really have any control over is when we die. At that time . . . and that time alone . . . we can just do as we damn well please."

Bruin frowned. "How do you figure? If you're dying, I'd think you'd be too damn sick to do much of anything. You could still get drunk and play a few hands of cards, but . . ."

"You're really missing my point," the boot maker said with great patience. "What I'm getting at is this . . . when you are dying, you can do anything you please and say anything you wish *because you have nothing left to lose*."

"Well," Bruin replied, "I pretty much say what I think to whoever I'm around when I'm healthy."

"Maybe you do and maybe you don't. But all I'm saying is

that, at death's doorstep, you can finally be completely honest."

"Hmm," Bruin mused, "I can see that you've put a lot of thought to this deathbed business."

"I have, and I am not afraid to put my theories to the test when my time is almost at hand. Until then, I'm thinking of writing a book about my liberating theories of death and dying."

"Well," Bruin said, starting to feel a bit uneasy. "If I was you, I'd stick to making good boots that are easy on a man's feet. Now I've given some serious thought to good leather, and I can tell you that a good boot is a worthy thing to make, and also that . . ."

"Good day, sir," the boot maker said rather abruptly. "And I hope you live to wear better boots than you're wearing right now because, frankly, they are pathetic."

Bruin gazed down at his boots and knew the man was right. The heels were worn to nubs and the soles were shot. Maggot had bitten the top off one boot in a fit of anger, and they both had been cut by brush and rocks until they were hardly fit to wear.

"Maybe I'll come back and have you fit me someday."

"I doubt that very much, but I would have one last word of advice," the little boot maker said in a solemn voice.

"And that would be?"

"Don't die with those boots on because it would be a disgrace."

"I guess it would," Bruin said, leaving the shop with his head spinning.

He was still in a daze when he rounded a corner and saw two men giving the Mogollon Apache family a hard time. Bruin pulled up short and stayed out of the way for a moment, sizing up the situation. From what he could tell, the Apache had been selling their antler wares and two large and belligerent men were trying to beat them down on their prices.

"Hellfire!" one of the men shouted, standing head and shoulders over Johnny and his wife. "You damned Indians think that your time is worth something when it ain't! I said I'd pay you twenty-five cents for that antler-knife handle and you're askin' a whole dollar."

"It's *worth* a dollar," Johnny said with firmness. "I spent a day cutting and shaping the handle and my wife spent two more days polishing. You won't find a nicer knife handle anywhere."

The other man scoffed and spat a stream of tobacco juice on Johnny's pants. "What you don't seem to realize, you ignorant Apache trash, is that we could just take the damn handle . . . take all of 'em in fact . . . and there wouldn't be a thing you or your squaw could do to stop us."

"Go away," Nana said, coming to the defense of her parents.

"Yes," Camila added, "why don't you go back into the saloon and drink more whiskey."

Bruin was too late to prevent the bigger of the pair from backhanding Camila so hard that she was knocked completely off her feet. Johnny and his wife both attacked, but were also battered and then hurled to the ground. Nana grabbed a knife and dashed forward to stab one of the attackers in the leg, but the other man hit her in the face so hard she dropped like a stone.

Bruin gave no warning as he closed distance. He did not think about his broken ribs when he struck the larger man with such force that it cracked his jawbone, twisting his face in a clownish grin. The second man twisted around just in time to have his teeth almost shoved down his throat. The man spat his front teeth a good twenty feet into the air, and let out a scream that could have been heard in Flagstaff. Bruin hit him a second time, turning his nose to tomato sauce an instant before he landed facedown in the dust.

"Nana!" Judith cried, running to her daughter.

Bruin hurried over to kneel beside the girl and her badly shaken parents. Bruin could see that Nana was unconscious but breathing. "We'll get her to a doctor."

"We don't have any money for a doctor!" Johnny exclaimed.

"I do," Bruin said, scooping Nana up and turning to Camila. "Let's go!"

They hurried up the street to a doctor's office, and after Nana was giving smelling salts, she revived, but her face was already swelling. Camila also had a terrible bruise, and her Apache parents looked beside themselves with anxiety.

"I'll go back and kill 'em both," Bruin said as soon as he knew that the Apache family were in competent hands. "Doc, how much do I owe you for your services?"

"Five dollars."

Bruin paid the man and started off to break some arms and legs, but Johnny and Judith stopped him at the door, pleading for the enraged giant not to hurt the two bullies any more.

"They were drunk," Judith said. "Jesus Christ says we need to forgive them and turn the other cheek."

"I think different times call for different circumstances," Bruin argued. "What you must do in this day and age is bust up ornery sonofabitches like that pair in order to teach them civil manners."

"You're right," Johnny said, wiping blood from his smashed lips and reaching for his sheath knife.

"Don't be crazy," Judith cried. "We must live the Christian way. There's been enough violence. We'll just go back and get our goods and then leave Pine River because the whites will blame us . . . not that pair. And we can't allow our anger to cause other Apache to suffer."

"You didn't do anything but protect yourselves," Bruin said, seeing the woman's point but refusing to bend from his anger.

"Mr. Henry," the doctor said. "The reservation Apache in these parts already face a lot of anger and hatred. I think these people are right and that you should drop any thought of further punishment, even though I am furious at the idea of grown men hitting women and children."

"Okay," Bruin said grudgingly. "But, if that pair are brought here for your services, I hope you ain't gentle."

"Believe me, I won't be. Did you hurt them bad?"

"A broken jaw and nose. Maybe more. I hit them real hard."

"Then I'm sure they got the worst of it," the doctor said. "It might be best if you and this family leave Pine River for a while."

"Will the girls be all right?"

"They'll be fine. There are no broken bones in their faces, and the swelling will go down in a few days. Children are tougher than we think."

Bruin thought of Ophelia and knew the doctor was right. He paid the man and then excused himself, knowing he needed to take a long walk to cool his anger down. An hour later, he ended up at the livery expecting to find Ophelia. She would be very upset upon learning that the two Apache girls her own age had been struck so hard along with their parents. And she'd want to go running off to find Link.

Bruin understood that, but he sure didn't see the point in chasing after her father. It was as clear as the sky overhead that Link had duped this entire town into thinking he was a legitimate and honest lawman. The only question in Bruin's mind was if he had already killed his deputies and the four men who had robbed the bank so that he could enjoy all the stolen money.

Ophelia wasn't at the livery as he'd expected, so Bruin found a pile of clean straw bedding and took another short nap. He was tired, and supposed it was due to the pain in his ribs and the fact that he never did sleep well inside a room.

When he awoke, the sun was past its zenith and he guessed it was at least two o'clock. Bruin brushed the straw from his clothes and hunted up the man who owned the livery.

"You seen that girl that I came in with on the medicine wagon? We were supposed to meet here around noon."

"I ain't seen her today, but she came back shortly after you talked to the blacksmith about fixing that bad wagon wheel."

"Yeah, I was supposed to get it yesterday by five o'clock, but I forgot."

"The blacksmith worked hard on that wheel and had it ready. He's still going to expect his twenty dollars."

Bruin wasn't surprised that the liveryman knew about their little financial arrangement. The two businesses were located almost on top of each other. "I'll pay him what I agreed. What were you saying about the girl?"

"As soon as her palomino mare was grained and watered, she rode out of here with a bag of food and her bedroll."

"What!"

The liveryman took a backward step. "I said the girl left in a hurry not long after the pair of you arrived yesterday."

Bruin's knees almost buckled. "Where did she go?" he asked, knowing exactly where she went . . . to find her father.

"Headed up the street going north. Said something about looking for her father."

"But how'd she think she could do that by herself!"

"Well," the liveryman said, looking sheepish, "I did tell her about an old Apache that used to be an Army scout and tracker. He is still one of the best and gets hired to track people and animals. Lives about two miles north of here in an old rock house on the right hand of the road. The girl sounded excited about hiring him and said she had plenty of gold."

"That part is true enough," Bruin groused. "What's the old Apache's name?"

"Yanzi."

Bruin was fit to be tied. "Can he be trusted?"

"I believe so, especially if he's fairly paid and treated. I've never heard anyone speak ill of the man. He doesn't speak much English but he's smart and once you put him on someone's trail, he'll stick until he's got whoever you're looking for in sight."

"I know him," Johnny said, coming up from where he'd been listening. "And he's one of my tribe. We speak the same language."

"You speak Apache?"

"Not as good as English, but enough to understand. My wife and I preach to the Apache and have made a few converts." Johnny asked why the girl was looking for Link, and when Bruin took him aside and explained the situation, the Apache said, "We had better leave now."

"What about your wife and girls?"

"They can come too."

But Bruin shook his head. "We've got a lot of time to make up. We'll be traveling too fast for them to keep up on foot."

"They'll catch us when we catch your granddaughter."

Bruin was in too much of a hurry to argue the point. "I'll get you fixed up with a horse and . . ."

"No," Johnny said. "I will run."

"Run?"

"Yes," the Apache said, "I can keep up with any mule."

Bruin figured that was probably true, so he didn't say another word as he hurried off to find and saddle Maggot.

TWENTY-ONE

—⚊⚊—

IT HADN'T TAKEN very long for Ophelia to find the Apache's small rock house and the attached shed where he kept hay, grain, and an old Army saddle. Ophelia noticed that there was also a pole corral containing a handsome sorrel gelding guarded by two huge hounds.

When the dogs saw Ophelia and the mare, they set up a terrible racket. By the time that she reached Yanzi's front door, the yapping hounds were on their back heels fighting at the chains that held them bound.

The Apache was taller than Johnny, but weighed less. He had long, wispy hair silver in color and tied behind the nape of his skinny, wrinkled neck. His skin was the color of old leather and just as cracked and dry. He wore a faded Army tunic with a sergeant's strips half torn away, moccasins, and leather leggings. A bowie knife rested in a beaded sheath, and Yanzi held his baggy pants up with a pair of bright red suspenders.

Ophelia had never seen such an interesting man. "My name is Ophelia Cochran," she began, still mounted on the palomino. "I have come to hire you to help find my father, Marshal Link Cochran. He and two deputies have gone after four bank robbers. I have learned that they stole five thousand dollars. But neither my father, his deputies, or the robbers have been seen since leaving Pine River."

Yanzi listened nodding his head every now and then the way he had learned to do from his years tracking for the United States Army. His eyes were dark brown, his face composed, and he wore an expression that made the white speakers think he not only understood their long explanations, but cared about them.

The girl talked with great excitement, and he thought she was pretty but rattled and confused. Yanzi couldn't really hear the girl very well because his ears had been damaged by too many rifle shots, and then there were his pair of noisy hounds.

When the girl stopped talking, Yanzi held out his hand for money. If the girl had money, he would take the next step, which was to make sign language and learn what she really wanted him to do. Perhaps she wanted only to buy the noisy dogs or his fine sorrel. He would get money first, and the rest would happen later.

When Ophelia saw the Apache's outstretched hand, she realized that Yanzi not understood a word she had spoken. And now, he wanted to be paid. What nerve to waste her breath and precious time!

Ophelia wanted to ride away without the Apache's help, but knew she could not. Swallowing her impatience, she found her pouch with the gold nuggets and selected a pea-sized one to place in Yanzi's hand.

He studied the nugget and then he put it into his mouth. Ophelia watched as he bit into the nugget as if it were candy. She could not help but notice that Yanzi was missing most of his front teeth, but she supposed he had back teeth for chewing.

The Apache removed the nugget and studied the imprints

of his worn molars before he grinned and said, "Thank you, white eyes."

"I need you to find my father."

He sagely nodded, and then watched as she began to make crude sign language, which he considered quite the worst he had ever witnessed. At first, he thought that the excited girl needed to relieve herself, and he pointed to the bushes behind his shed. Then, he realized that her going-away motions meant that she wanted to find him someone important.

Yanzi frowned and pointed in all directions, and when Ophelia shrugged, he understood that she didn't even know where to start. This was troubling because, while Yanzi thought of himself the best tracker alive, he was not possessed of visions.

For a long moment, they stood looking at each other, and then Ophelia said in a slow and distinct voice, "My father is a missing officer of the law."

Now Yanzi understood better, and knelt to draw a circle in the dirt. Ophelia knelt too, and pointed at an imaginary spot in the circle and said, "Pine River."

"Good," Yanzi said.

"Here is where they went," she explained, drawing a line to the north and pointing that way with her finger. "Seven men."

To make sure that Yanzi really understood, Ophelia held up seven fingers. Four on one hand while making a face and trying to mimic a theft, and then three on the other hand saying, "United States marshal. Lawmen."

Then, hoping to make her explanation even clearer, Ophelia had three fingers chasing four fingers to the north. If the situation had been different, her absurd mimicking would have made her giggle.

Yanzi finally thought he understood. A robber and a posse had ridden north, but now were missing. His job was to find them, and he believed the job could not have been easier. Seven white men would leave a trail even a blind man could follow. After all, he had spent most of his Army time tracking cunning Apache fighters including the Chiricahua, Mescalero, and the Jicarilla raiders who still terrorized the white settlers in New Mexico. The nugget was very valuable, and Yanzi was glad that this girl did not want to buy his horse or hounds. Ophelia had paid him well, shown him respect, and was clearly eager to find the seven white men.

The Apache went inside the rock house, where he gathered a little corn and beans as well as his rifle and pistol, both gifts from the Army in gratitude for his years of dangerous and faithful military service. Yanzi dumped everything outside, and then tied his hounds beside his door so that they would discourage thieves.

"I don't know what I would have done if you hadn't been here," Ophelia said as the tracker saddled his horse with a McClellan saddle that had heavy oak stirrups with leather covers. She watched with interest as Yanzi stuffed packages of food and ammunition in two leather pouches along with a round Army canteen. Ophelia also noticed that Yanzi's rifle was a big Spencer and his pistol an Army Colt.

"I don't expect we'll be in need of weapons," Ophelia said, showing him that she carried a .36 Navy Colt in her own saddlebags. "But I suppose it's good to be prepared for the worst."

Yanzi led the sorrel gelding over to a stump and mounted his fine horse with care. Then, without waiting for Ophelia, he galloped north as if he knew exactly where to find the tracks of seven desperate men.

TWO HOURS LATER and far from the road, the Apache was on his hands and knees, crabbing around in the brush. Ophelia had tried to ask him questions concerning what he was doing and planned to do, but Yanzi ignored her and seemed so intent on his tracking that she had given up any attempt to satisfy her curiosity.

Finally, the tracker stood and pointed to a gap in the mountains. Ophelia stood in her stirrups and leaned forward, as if she could will herself closer to her father. She was filled with anxiety concerning his safety. What if Link had been ambushed, despite Bruin's assurances otherwise? After all, anyone could make a mistake, and her father was no longer a young man. He might even be suffering from a diminishment of his eyesight.

Ophelia could not bear to think of her father lying dead or dying in some brush-choked gully or perhaps along a mountain trail. And it was all that she could do to bite her tongue in order not to speak sharply at the Apache because he was wasting so much time on the ground when they should be hurrying along on horseback.

Yanzi remounted and pushed on as the evening shadows lengthened and the sun began to set in the west. Ophelia felt exhausted, for she had not slept a wink the night before when Bruin was hurt and they were afraid that Marshal Kilpatrick might suddenly appear. She yawned and calculated that she had been awake for more than thirty-six anxiety-ridden hours. But any physical discomfort or mental anguish would be as nothing if her father was still alive.

When darkness fell, the Apache tracker unsaddled and then grained his horse before he cooked a mush of beans and corn meal. Yanzi motioned for Ophelia to eat his food, but she declined. The mush looked ghastly and her stomach was acting rebellious. She did have some old hard rock candy from Flagstaff, and chewed it slowly, then wrapped herself in her horse blanket and studied the fire, thinking about all that had happened to her since leaving Prescott as a criminal on the run.

Mostly, Ophelia sorrowed for the loss of her mother. They had been close for so many years, always leaning on each other in times of trial. Her mother had really been more like a big sister, a much wiser big sister. But toward the end, when she was so sick and in pain all the time, Ophelia had begun to pray for Kate to be released to heaven. Now, as Ophelia's eyelids drooped, she chose to believe that Kate was an angel hovering just outside the firelight, somewhere up in the pines, or even along the crests of the mountains, always watching over her daughter.

Ophelia had no fear of sleeping near the Apache. Something about him told her that he was a good man, although he was as hard and as enduring a cedar tree. She was comforted by Yanzi's calm presence, although she greatly missed Bruin Henry. That realization came as a surprise because Ophelia had not considered the fact that they had become emotionally attached.

Ophelia reminded herself that Bruin was a bloody and a violent man. That he had killed often and without remorse and that he was no Christian. He was fearsome to the extreme, and yet, when they had come upon the diseased settlement, Ophelia had felt his sadness despite the fact that those who had died were thieves and worse. Also, she knew that her grandfather loved her and mourned deeply for his daughter, now buried in Prescott.

But that being the case, why hadn't Bruin helped her and her mother in their times of need? Ophelia did not know, and yet even as she asked this question, she asked herself why her own father had been absent almost all of her life. Like Bruin Henry, why hadn't he come to help during all those many difficult years?

Ophelia tried not to judge Bruin or her father, but she couldn't help but feel that they had wronged both herself and her mother. Ophelia promised herself that, if she found her father alive tomorrow, she would summon up the courage to ask him why he hadn't come to help his wife and daughter.

Her eyes closed, and she listed to the sounds of night animals out in the deep forest. She heard their picketed horses, and remembered the great white mule that Bruin so loved. What an ornery critter Maggot was!

The Apache tracker said something, and Ophelia's eyes popped open. But he was rocking on his blanket next to the fire and offering prayers or perhaps singing some Indian song.

Ophelia had no idea what he was singing, and given the gravity of what they might find tomorrow, she realized that it really didn't matter.

IT WAS COLD and cloudy when Yanzi awoke her early the next morning. His campfire offered little warmth, but this time when he offered her a portion of pale yellow mush, she managed to eat. Ophelia would have loved some of Bruin Henry's strong, early morning coffee. She had gotten used to its kick, which always knocked the sleep from her brain. Now, however, she was wide awake and wondering what this day might bring. She knew that her father and his deputies could be many, many miles away, but hoped they were not. Ophelia wasn't even sure that she would recognize Link Cochran or he would recognize her given how many years had passed since he'd visited Prescott. And how would her father react when he learned that his wife had died and that Bruin had come to kneel and mourn beside her deathbed?

But the most troubling question of all had to do with her father and grandfather being mortal enemies. Ophelia could not bring herself to believe that this was so. Surely they could settle their differences and become friends. Surely they could forget the past and look to the future. And so, as she gulped down Yanzi's tasteless yellow mush, Ophelia said a little prayer that her father and grandfather would not soon kill one another.

The Apache grained, then saddled and bridled their horses. Ophelia noticed that he was stiff when he mounted, and she wondered how many Army campaigns he had ridden against his own people. Had Yanzi helped the famous Indian agent John Clum arrest Geronimo years ago and then escort him to the San Carlos Indian Reservation, which was less than a hundred miles to the south? And after Geronimo went on the warpath again, terrorizing Northern Mexico and all of the Southwest, had Yanzi ridden under General George Crook to again track the infamous raider down and force him to surrender?

Ophelia couldn't help but watch the tracker with growing interest, wishing they spoke the same language so she could learn what she was sure would be an incredible tale.

Yanzi rode out of camp acting like a man who was alone. He wasted no time in picking up the trail, and Ophelia realized that they were now deep in the wild and uncharted Mogollon Rim forest. They saw deer, elk, wild turkeys, and, around mid-morning, vultures circling in the sky. Yanzi looked up often at the vultures, and as Ophelia tried to keep her mare close behind the Apache, she could not help but wonder at his thoughts. She felt an urgency in the way Yanzi was now pushing his sorrel gelding, and it made her more and more afraid of what they soon might find.

About noon, Yanzi suddenly drew rein and dismounted. Ophelia started to ask him what was wrong, but he raised one hand and clamped the other over his mouth telling her to be silent. Ophelia dismounted, heart pounding. The vultures were circling very low, and she could hear their squawking and hissing.

The Apache stopped in mid-stride, and then slowly tied his horse to a tree. Ophelia did the same. She knew that Yanzi had come upon something terrible because of the gathering of vultures, and she was so afraid that it might be her father and his deputies that she wanted to vomit.

Yanzi motioned her forward, and Ophelia discovered that her legs had turned to stone. The Apache came back to help her, and when they peeked through the thick brush and trees, Ophelia did vomit and then she fainted.

She awoke when the Apache poured water from his canteen onto her face and then clamped his rough hand over her mouth. His eyes told her more clearly than words that there were dead men ahead. The only question was . . . was one of them her poor missing father?

TWENTY-TWO

—◆—

OPHELIA DIDN'T REMEMBER walking trancelike down into the field and the sweet stench of death. She heard but did not comprehend as the old Apache tracker picked up rocks and hurled them at the vultures, driving them away with their hooked and blood-dripping beaks.

She counted six dead men, two of them still wearing deputy's badges. They had been shot to pieces, and from the looks on what remained of their faces, caught totally by surprise. A dying campfire still smoldered and emitted a thin wisp of smoke. There were nervous horses still tied to a picket line, eyes rolling up at the noisy flesh-eating birds again circling overhead.

Yanzi made Ophelia sit on a rock, and she watched but did not really see as he picked his way around the campfire, examining each man, two of whom were still wrapped in their bedrolls with their missing eyeballs and cheeks spattered with blood. Yanzi also searched their saddlebags and belongings, finding only a few cheap pocket watches and a derringer.

Father, Ophelia cried silently again and again. *Father!*

Suddenly, she jumped up from the rock and stumbled over to stare into frozen dead faces one by one, until she knew that her father was still alive. That he was the seventh man. She also realized that this camp was attacked at sunrise, and that these men had been shot to death before they could reach for their own guns or gather their wits.

Once certain that her father was not one of the six dead men, Ophelia staggered back to her horse. She untied the now-frightened mare and mounted her, then started to ride around the death camp.

"Whoa!" the Apache shouted, jolting her out of a daze. "Whoa!"

He grabbed her mare's reins and stared into Ophelia's eyes for a moment before she held up one trembling finger.

Yanzi held out his hand too, and Ophelia understood enough to give him another gold nugget. Yanzi bit it, and this time he did not grin as he remounted the sorrel.

Ophelia knew then that he was going to find her father and that, when they found Link Cochran, there would be many difficult questions for him to answer. Questions even harder than why he had abandoned his wife and daughter in Prescott. Questions about his two murdered deputies and the four bank robbers as well as five thousand dollars.

THE TRACK OF the lone rider was easy to follow, and even Ophelia could see from the way that the hoofprints cupped the forest floor that her father was in a big hurry. Was he chasing the assassin who had killed his deputies and the bank robbers? Or was *he* the assassin who had murdered them all and taken the stolen bank money?

Ophelia didn't want Yanzi to know if it turned out that her father was a killer and thief. As they hurried along, Ophelia wished she could simply tell the Apache that it had all been a mistake and that they could quit the hunt. She would let him keep the second gold nugget with her blessings, but please . . .

please, don't let him find out that her father had murdered those six men.

Ophelia could not tell the Apache these things, and so they rushed on through the heavy forest, ducking branches, yanking their horses' heads up as they slipped and stumbled on rocks and decaying wood. The day went on and on like a nightmare, and Ophelia was oblivious to fresh saddle sores. She felt numb physically as well as mentally. What had happened back there where the vultures gathered over human flesh? What unspeakable crime might her father have committed?

At the end of the day, Yanzi dismounted and again placed his hand over his mouth to indicate the importance of absolute silence. That's when Ophelia realized she was finally about to meet her father. She knew it in the anguished turmoil of her mind, and she knew it in the deepest aching marrow of her bones.

A cabin in a grassy meadow with a single horse tied outside and smoke rising from a rock chimney is what Ophelia saw, and all that she allowed her mind to grasp.

She waited beside the Apache and watched as evening shadows darkened the meadow, and didn't know what to do next. Ophelia knew that her father was in the cabin. And try as she might, she believed that he was holding five thousand dollars and with no possible excuses for not returning to his office in Pine River.

What should she do? Leave without any answers? Sneak away with the tracker and go back to find Bruin and tell him that he was right all along about her father? Ophelia didn't know what to do now that the moment of truth was at hand. She wanted to leave, and yet that was impossible because Ophelia knew that she could not live the rest of her life with so many unanswered questions.

"Go back," she blurted out without preamble.

The Apache shook his head and drew his rifle from its scabbard.

"Please go back," she repeated, pushing the long barrel of

his rifle toward the pine needles at their feet. "Thank you. You have well earned your gold." And then, before he could stop her, Ophelia mounted her mare and sent it thundering down into the meadow that surrounded the old log cabin. Her father's horse whinnied long out of loneliness. The cabin door blew open and there stood her Link, a rifle balanced in his hands.

"Father! It's Ophelia!" she cried as he brought the rifle to his shoulder and prepared to fire. "It's me, Ophelia!"

Slowly, the rifle came down and Link stared with disbelief. Then Ophelia was leaping from the palomino and skidding to a stop.

"Ophelia?"

She hardly recognized her own father because he was far leaner than she remembered and his beard was silver. There were deep crow's feet at the corners of Link's eyes; his lips were lips thin and his face pale.

"What are you doing here?" he demanded, dragging her inside the cabin. "Who brought you?"

"Father," she cried, feeling his claws dig into her flesh. "You're hurting me!"

"Who!"

"An Apache tracker named Yanzi. But I sent him home. I'm alone. I had to find you!" She was crying like a baby, mad and confused all at the same time.

"Stop it!" he shouted, now studying the meadow she'd just raced across. "Are you *sure* that you're alone?"

"Yes!"

Finally, he relaxed. "You'd better be. How did you ever get here? Why did you come? What about your mother?"

"She's dead."

For the first time, Link's face softened. "What happened?"

"Mother died of a cancer. We buried her in Prescott weeks ago."

"Who is 'we'?"

"Grandpa Bruin Henry paid for the funeral. It was a fine funeral too. But the marshal there named Wade Kilpatrick,

well, we had to trick him and now he's after us. He knows that
Grandfather has discovered a vein of pure gold."

"Where?" Link asked, his voice much more friendly.

"In the Superstition Mountains. But that doesn't matter.
We've found you and . . . what happened back there where all
those men were murdered?"

He turned away from her and went over to his fire. He was
frying venison and something else, but Ophelia didn't care
and wasn't hungry. "Father, what happened to those six men!"

"They were . . . all shot."

"I know that. But . . ."

"We were jumped," he said miserably. "Jumped for the
money that was stolen from the bank at Pine River."

Ophelia was confused. "You mean that someone else is up
here?"

"Yeah," he said. "I'm after them. That's why I almost shot
you out of the saddle just now."

"How many men are you still hunting?"

"I don't know. They hit us at daybreak when the light was
poor. I was just lucky to get away with my life." Link shook
his head and bent over the fire to turn the sizzling venison
steaks. "Look, Ophelia, you shouldn't have come to find me.
I'm outnumbered and I don't need you to worry about. I can't
handle any more trouble than I'm already facing."

"Bruin Henry will be coming after me. He'll discover I've
left Pine River, and he'll be on his way here as sure as the sun
will rise tomorrow morning."

Link turned back to look at her. "Bruin is still alive, is he?"

"Yes. And I think he wants to apologize."

"Bruin Henry, apologize?" Link chuckled without humor.
"That's impossible."

"But he does!" Ophelia insisted. "He knows how he
messed your life up all those years ago during that Yuma stage
robbery. He's been paying for it ever since, and now, with the
gold he's discovered over in the Superstitions, Grandfather
wants to make amends."

Link rose to his feet. He was taller than Ophelia remembered, and although time and travel had left their marks on his face, he was still handsome and had that wonderful smile. "Is that a fact?"

"It is, and he's discovered enough gold to make his amends. I think . . . I think he's one day going to become a Christian like Mother and me."

The corners of Link's mouth lifted and he said, "Do tell."

"Yes, Father." To Ophelia's embarrassment, she began to cry again.

"Come here," he said, laying down the ladle and opening his arms.

She flew into his embrace and he whispered, "Ophelia, I have so much to tell you, and I want to begin by saying I'm sorry. Sorry for the father I never was, and sorry for the husband I should have been for your dear mother. I've tried to bring justice to this country, but in so doing, I've committed the greatest injustice of all . . . abandoning my family. It's too late to ask your mother to forgive me now, but I'm asking you. Can you ever forgive me?"

Could she ever! She rubbed her eyes dry with the back of her shirtsleeve and managed to say, "Grandpa was right when he said that there is no justice in this world."

"Yeah," Link said softly. "Bruin is right about that. And I promise you that I'll forgive him if he's forgiven me."

"Oh, he has!"

"That's fine news, Ophelia. Now, would you like something to eat? You're probably starved to death."

Ophelia *was* starving. She wanted to eat and talk and talk to her father, but for right now, she just wanted to be held in the cradle of his strong and loving arms.

TWENTY-THREE

—∞—

BRUIN HENRY REINED Maggot up in the trees overlooking the meadow. "That's Ophelia's mare," he said to Johnny. "She's inside with Link."

"That's what Yanzi said."

Bruin dismounted and tied Maggot to a tree. "I'm not sure what to do now," he confessed. "Link's horse is still there, so the pair of them must be inside, meaning I can't just open fire on the cabin."

"You need to talk to them," the Apache said. "Find out what they are going to do next."

Bruin nodded with agreement. He and Johnny had seen the death camp with the six bodies earlier that day, and it didn't take a genius to figure out that Link Cochran had double-crossed and then slaughtered his own men for the bank's money. And surely Ophelia must have realized that by now.

So what was going on down there?

Bruin turned to the Apache. "Johnny," he said, "I'm going down there alone. You stay hidden here and wait for your wife and girls to catch up. If I'm killed, can you shoot Link for me?"

"No," Johnny said, "I could not."

"But dammit, what if you saw the man about to shoot his daughter?"

The Apache thought a long time about this, and said, "Then I would shoot him dead, God forgive me."

"Glad to hear that," Bruin said, checking his weapons one more time. "Listen. There's one last thing I want you to know because I trust you."

The Apache waited.

"It's this," Bruin said. "If I get killed down there, I want you to follow Ophelia and her father until you're sure that she's going to be safe."

"We could do this."

"I've told Ophelia exactly where I discovered the gold. I even drew her a map figuring that, if something happened to me, I'd want her to have the gold. But if something happened to both Ophelia and me, then I'd want you and your family to have the gold. No use in letting it just sit there until some other prospector stumbles on it like I did."

"I don't want your gold."

"Don't say that," Bruin countered. "I know you think that money and gold are the source of most of our evils. But I'm convinced that it can also be used for good. So, I'm going to draw you a map same as I did Ophelia, and I want you to have that gold if everything goes wrong. I don't think Link would kill his own daughter, but he might. And he's sure likely to kill me."

Johnny said nothing as Bruin drew the Apache a map. "You could use this to help your family and your people. You could give some to the church or use it to buy food and stuff for orphan Apache kids. Hell, Johnny, if you put your mind to it, you could do all sorts of good and decent things with the gold in my claim."

"I couldn't file a legal claim on your gold. The white people would never let an Indian do that."

"I expect that you are right. So you'd just have to work the claim until it was played out. But with your wife and daughters, you could do that." Bruin handed him the map and explained the details before saying, "I never thought I'd do something like this, but I know that you and your family are good, honest people and you deserve a break."

"Thank you," the Apache said.

"Just . . . just try to watch out for Ophelia if I get shot."

Johnny nodded. "I will offer a prayer for your safety."

"Appreciate it," Bruin said, giving the surprised Apache a big hug. "I want you to know that, if we'd found Link Cochran dead, I'd have asked you and your family to partner up with me and Ophelia on the gold. I'd already decided to do that, Johnny."

Bruin guessed that there was little else to say except? "And if I get killed down there at the cabin, I want you to also take care of Maggot. He deserves to be put out to pasture and left in peace. He's a good mule, even though he has a bad temperament. Maggot can't be faulted for not liking people . . . hell, I don't like most folks myself."

"Be careful, Bruin Henry."

"I will. My main worry is for Ophelia. I've lived my life, and it don't much matter at this stage of the game what happens to me. But it's different with my granddaughter. She's got a lot of living left to do . . . same as Nana and Camila."

"I will take care of her and your mule if I have to," Johnny promised as Bruin rode out of the trees and down into the meadow.

"HE'S HERE!" OPHELIA cried from inside the cabin where she had been watching for her grandfather.

Link smiled. "Good. Your grandfather and I are going to have to have a few words in private before we go anywhere. Maybe you should stay here out of sight."

"I won't interrupt," Ophelia said, "but I'm not going to

stay hidden. If I'm here with you both, I don't think you'll kill each other."

"All right," Link said. "Just make sure that Bruin doesn't go for his gun, or I'll have to go for mine and I'm a lot faster than he is. I don't want to have to kill that old man if his heart has changed about me."

"It has," Ophelia promised. "Just let me go out to meet him and tell him that everything will be all right."

"I expect that would be the thing to do," Link agreed. "I'll be watching from just inside the door. You tell that old man to keep his hands empty and in plain sight."

"I will."

"Tell him that, if he even looks like he's going to reach for a gun or a rifle, I'll shoot him dead."

"I will . . . but he won't."

"Make sure of it, Ophelia. It's all on your shoulders."

She knew that her father was right. Knew full well how the two men had hated each other for so many years. And now nothing mattered except that they made their peace.

Ophelia rushed out of the cabin and started walking toward Bruin and Maggot. They looked so big together, and so brave, that she had to bite her lip to keep from getting upset. She was sure that she could make a peace between the two men who mattered most in her life and she would do it right now.

"Hello, Ophelia," he said when they were near.

"Hello, Bruin."

"He's inside with a gun trained on me, isn't he."

"Yes, but he's promised not to shoot. I told him that you wanted to bury the hatchet and end the feud. I told him that I wanted you and my father to be friends more than anything in the world."

Bruin lifted his eyes to the log cabin. "I doubt that is possible, Child."

"Try!"

Bruin took a deep breath. "I met Yanzi coming back to Pine River. He told me about the death camp, and then I saw those six dead men with my own eyes. Your father double-crossed that bunch and then took the bank money for himself."

"No, he didn't!" Ophelia swallowed hard. "He told me what really happened. He and his deputies were in charge, but got jumped at dawn. Somehow, my father managed to escape with his life, and the ambushers took all the bank money and whatever cash they could find on the bodies."

"And you believe that?"

"Yes. I've had time to search the cabin and my father's things. There's no money, and he wants to go after the men who attacked his camp. He's planning to go alone, but I told him that we'd help."

Bruin listened with amazement. He thought to try and convince Ophelia that her father was a clever and cunning man along with being a skilled liar. But what good would his words do when this girl was so determined not to see the truth of the matter? There seemed to be only one thing to do, and that was to go along with the lie until Link himself exposed the truth.

"I'll help him catch those killers," Bruin heard himself say.

"You will?"

"I just said that I would."

Ophelia jumped forward with a cry of happiness. She startled Maggot, who whirled and nearly unseated Bruin before he kicked out at her but missed.

"Easy, mule!" Bruin said angrily. "You kick Ophelia and I swear I'll shoot you between the eyes!"

"It's all right," Ophelia said, realizing how close she'd come to being hurt or killed. One kick in the head from that huge Missouri mule and she'd be a goner. "It was my fault for startling him."

Bruin dismounted. "Let's get this over with and meet your father."

"He's changed a lot," Ophelia warned. "He looks far older than I expected, and there's a hardness in him now very much like the hardness you carry inside."

"I don't carry any hardness inside."

"Yes, you do," Ophelia said. "But it's forgiven because I know that you have a good heart, same as Father."

"If he tries to kill me when we meet, I will defend myself as best I can."

"He won't!"

"We'll see about that," Bruin told her. He dropped his reins to the ground and said to Maggot, "Stay right here where I put you and don't move or you might catch a stray bullet."

"Bruin, don't talk like that."

"Can't help it. A viper might shed its skin and even change its color a bit, but it's still a viper. I reckon the same can be said for Link Cochran."

Ophelia sighed. "If you try to kill my father I'll . . . I'll never trust another human being again. I mean that, Grandfather Henry."

Bruin looked into her eyes and knew that was the truth, and that it would be a scar this girl would carry for the rest of her life.

"All right," he said, "I will act in good faith towards your father."

"That's all that I ask," she said as she took his big paw in her own and led him toward the cabin.

Link stepped outside with his right hand dangling close to his six-gun. "Well, what have we here? Bruin Henry, I do believe, looking as old as Moses."

"You've aged hard yourself," Bruin growled.

"The only reason that I haven't killed you in the last minute or two is because my daughter has promised me that you have seen the light, so to speak. That you no longer intend to kill me."

"That's about right."

"So are we going to be friends for Ophelia's sake?"

"I guess that's it."

"Good," Link said. "I need your help in recovering the bank money." His voice grew cold. "You saw what the ambushers did to my deputies and prisoners. They're ruthless and have to be stopped."

"How many men jumped that camp?" Bruin asked, playing the man's lying game.

"I don't know. At least four. Will you and Ophelia ride to help me?"

"I'd rather my granddaughter go back to Pine River and wait for us."

"That's not in her best interest," Link said smoothly. "Now that we're all friends and family again, we need to stick together. When we get close to the ones that have the bank money, we can send Ophelia off so that her life is not in danger."

"You're calling the shots this time," Bruin grated.

"Glad you understand that." Link motioned past Bruin toward the trees. "Where are your friends?"

"The Apache have gone back to Pine River."

"How do I know that's true and that they aren't getting ready to ambush me?"

"You'll just have to take my word for it. They're a Christian family opposed to killing."

"Father, he's telling the truth."

"He'd better be because, if I see anyone out there, I'll shoot Bruin and ask questions later."

Ophelia paled but said nothing.

"Let's saddle up and go after those men," Link said. "Time is wasting."

"Where are they headed?" Bruin asked.

There was a pause, then Link said, "Southwest."

"Toward Phoenix and the Salt River Valley?"

"Yeah."

Bruin didn't dare smile or betray his true feelings. "And toward the Superstition Mountains?"

Link nodded. "I guess they'd be in that same direction. Hopefully, though, we can overtake them before they get too far into the desert."

Bruin nodded. "Might be a good idea."

"Can that white mule keep up with our horses?"

"He's a little played out," Bruin said. "Your horses have

had a day's rest, but he's been moving fast since we left Pine River."

"Make him keep up or we'll have to find you a horse," Link said as he turned his back and headed inside the cabin.

Right then, had it not been for his granddaughter, Bruin would have shot the viper in the back and told himself he had done the world a big favor. But since Ophelia was watching, there was nothing he could do but to go mount his white mule and see what happened on the road to his gold in the rugged Superstitions.

TWENTY-FOUR

—◦◦◦—

THE AMBUSHERS THAT Link claimed to be chasing down hadn't even left tracks to follow. Bruin wondered if Ophelia noticed this during their hard-riding days spent descending from the Mogollon Rim before crossing the northwest corner of the San Carlos Indian Reservation. When they reached the Salt River, Link led them into the hot country that Bruin knew well. He had prospected every square mile of this rugged, inhospitable desert, and he saw a hundred places where he could have killed Link had he been an ambusher.

Ophelia felt herself wither in the heat and tension that stretched sharp as a knife blade between her father and grandfather. She finally understood that they would never even like each other, much less be friends, and that realization made her feel both sad and angry. The two men never even spoke to each other except when it was absolutely necessary, and Ophelia knew that they had not abandoned their blood vendetta.

The temperature was over a hundred degrees when they rode across Horse Mesa. They were short on food, but then her father saw a distant movement in the brush and in less than a heartbeat, he yanked his rifle to his shoulder and fired, killing an antelope.

"Your eye is still sharp," Bruin said with grudging admiration. "I could barely even see that little antelope and you hit him on the run at well over a hundred and fifty yards."

"I can shoot a sparrow out of the sky," Link bragged. "And I haven't lost anything with my side arm either. That might be worth remembering, Bruin."

"I'll remember."

They were so hungry that they butchered the thin antelope and burned it over a brush fire even though there was no shade or water to make a decent camp. There was little left but entrails, hide, and bone when they remounted and continued deeper into the desert. Bruin occasionally sneaked a backward glance, but he didn't see anyone. Maybe the Apache family had decided to stay up on the Mogollon Rim, where the air was cool and scented with pine. Bruin couldn't blame them if they had, for this desert country punished both man and animal. Furthermore, it was crawling with poisonous scorpions, Gila monsters, and rattlesnakes.

On the following morning, when they were mounting up to leave just after daybreak, Link casually announced, "I think the killers we follow are headed toward the Superstitions."

"That would be my guess too," Bruin told him, knowing their deadly game was nearly over. "I wouldn't mind going over there and making sure that my claim hasn't been disturbed."

Link frowned as though this was a difficult request to grant. "I don't want to lose track of the men that killed my deputies and stole the bank's money."

"No," Bruin said with a straight face, "we wouldn't want to do that."

"On the other hand," Link quickly added, "it's clear that we've temporarily lost their trail, and we could just as easily find it in the Superstitions. That would be a pretty good place for outlaws to hide out, wouldn't it?"

"It would be," Bruin agreed, wondering why they even

bothered to keep up this nonsense, and then reminding himself it was all for Ophelia.

"All right. How far is it to your gold mine?"

"Less than twenty miles. It's close to the base of Superstition Peak."

"Twenty miles is nothing," Link told him. "We might as well see your gold mine, and we can reach it before sundown."

"It isn't a mine. Just a claim that I never had the time to file over in Prescott."

Link's eyebrows lifted in question. "So it's not even legally in your name?"

"Nope," Bruin assured the man. "But it will be if I ever get back to Prescott."

"Glad to hear that, old-timer!"

Bruin didn't like being called and "old-timer," but he was careful not to object. Twenty miles from now, when they were standing over his gold discovery, Link would try to kill him. That's when Ophelia would finally understand that her father was a liar and a heartless murderer.

OPHELIA DIDN'T KNOW what was going on . . . or maybe she didn't want to face up to the truth. But it seemed more and more likely that something very bad was going to happen when they got into the Superstition Mountains and found Bruin Henry's gold. She had a pistol in her saddlebags, and more than once, Bruin had stopped along their long trail together and insisted she practice firing the weapon. Ophelia knew she was still a poor shot, but she also knew that she could hit a large, still target five shots out of six. If one of her men tried to kill the other, she feared that she might have to use that gun.

"THERE IT IS," Bruin said, raising his hand to shield his eyes from the setting sun. "That's where my gold is to be found."

Link tipped the brim of his hat down low. "Where?"

"See that big boulder at the base of that cliff?"

"Yeah."

"The vein of pure gold runs under that boulder and into the face of the cliff. I've covered it up as best I could, but you'll easily find it now that you know exactly where to look. "

"You think anyone found it while you were gone?" Link asked, suddenly anxious.

"That's possible. There are a lot of prospectors in these mountains."

"Then let's go see if it's still there!" Link shouted, spurring his horse into a hard run over rocks and cactus.

Bruin let the man race on ahead at breakneck speed. Ophelia glanced over at him. "Grandpa, what's going to happen now?"

"You sure you want to know?"

"Tell me the truth."

"Your father is going to kill me if my gold hasn't been found."

"And what if it's been picked clean?"

"I don't know," Bruin admitted. "I expect your father will try and kill me anyway."

"And you'll try to kill him first?"

"That's my plan," Bruin confessed. "I may be old, but I've got some time left, and I ain't handing it over to Link Cochran without a fight."

Ophelia could barely speak through her trembling lips. "Isn't there *anything* that I can do or say to stop one of you from killing the other?"

"No, child, there isn't other than to pray. And the next best you can do is to forgive the one that survives and try to give yourself a chance at inner peace."

"But I don't want *either* one of you dead!"

"Sorry, Ophelia, but it can't be helped."

They both watched Link jump from his horse, race ahead on foot, and then push his shoulder against the massive boulder. Bruin was almost hoping at that moment his claim had been cleaned out and the gold all taken so that Ophelia's heart wouldn't get broken when he killed her father.

"It's here!" Link shouted, his voice shrill with excitement. He fell to his knees, found a pocket knife, and began to scrape furiously at the vein of pure gold. "My Gawd, it's got to be worth a fortune!"

"Ophelia, you've put me in a hard, hard spot. If I don't try to kill your father first, I'm a dead man. He's far quicker than me and a considerably better shot."

"I won't let him kill you," she said in a voice that Bruin could barely hear over Link's exuberant whoops and hollers. "But I can't let you kill him either."

"So where does that leave us?"

"Grandpa, please just ride away now!"

Bruin was not sure that he'd heard Ophelia correctly. "You want me to turn my back on a gold strike that took me seventeen years to find?"

"If you do that, then I'll really know for sure that your heart has changed and your greed is gone. And I'll know that I'm even more important to you than gold."

"But . . . but, Ophelia, that ain't fair! Don't you know that it was your father who killed those six men and took the bank's money? And that even five thousand bank dollars isn't enough and that he'll kill me . . . and maybe even you . . . for the gold he's just found?"

"I still don't know that about my father for certain," she whispered, "but I'm about to find out."

She took a deep, ragged breath. "Grandpa, I've never asked you for a favor. But this time, I'm *begging* you to turn Maggot around and leave behind a killing."

Bruin drew his sleeve across his sweaty brow and choked down bitter bile rising. He wanted to tell Ophelia that, if he couldn't have the gold, at least someone good like Johnny and his family ought to have it.

But Ophelia's eyes froze Bruin's tongue, and he couldn't bring himself to deny her. If he rode away right now it would finally prove to his granddaughter that his heart was good and that *she* . . . not the gold . . . was his most important thing in the whole world.

"I . . . I love you, child. Good-bye."

And then he was reining Maggot around and riding away. Bruin didn't know why he was doing such a fool thing, other than that he hadn't been able to deny Kate her deathbed wish and neither could he deny Ophelia her most fervent wish.

I'm a weak man, he thought. *Old, weak and a fool. And poor again.*

He had not ridden a hundred yards when the three tightly spaced rifle shots boomed and Maggot collapsed. Bruin threw himself across the thrashing white beast and yanked his own rifle free planning to either kill Link Cochran or be killed.

He was too late.

Wade Kilpatrick was standing on a rock not fifty feet from the gold claim looking triumphantly down at Link's body as he held a smoking rifle. Then Bruin's heart seized in his chest when he saw Ophelia racing toward her dead father. He tried to aim at Kilpatrick, but there was there so much sweat in Bruin's eyes that he knew he wouldn't be able to kill or even wound Prescott's ex-marshal.

He didn't need to.

More rifle shots split the hot desert air and echoed off the cliffs before Bruin could unleash his wild and hopeless shot at the former Prescott marshal. That's when Bruin saw Johnny and Yanzi lower their weapons as Kilpatrick tumbled from his rock perch like a broken doll, not stopping until he lay sprawled on the hot desert floor.

"Grandpa!" Ophelia cried as she raced to his side.

"Maggot's been hit," Bruin wailed as they hugged the white mule expecting to hear it expel its last fetid breath.

Maggot reared up and bit Bruin on the leg so hard the old giant threw back his head and howled. The mule tried to bite Ophelia too, but she was quicker and just managed to dodge his snapping jaws. The mule scrambled to its feet, ears back and yellow teeth gnashing in fury.

Bruin, still holding his mule-bitten leg, swore, "You ugly ingrate! Maggot, I hope you bleed to death!"

But the mule wouldn't bleed to death. The bullet had been deflected by Maggot's cinch ring and not one drop of his demented blood had been spilled.

A WEEK LATER, Bruin's vein of pure gold had all been extracted. Despite their highest hopes, there wasn't much more than ten thousand dollars worth to be taken, and yet, when Bruin thought about it, that was five thousand for Ophelia and five thousand for Yanzi and the Apache family.

"It will do," Ophelia said, her eyes avoiding the rock mounds under which Link Cochran and Wade Kilpatrick lay buried. "We'll take the bank's money I found in Father's saddlebags back to Pine River, and then we'll return to Prescott."

"Not me," Bruin told her. "I'm snake bit on towns and ready to go back to prospecting again. Will you grubstake me, Ophelia?"

"I'll do better than that. I'll be your prospecting partner."

But he shook his head. "You need more schooling and to be taught good manners by ladies."

"Maybe so, but for now, I'm sticking with you, Grandpa. You're all the family I've got left, and now I know for sure that your heart is true."

Bruin wanted to tell her that he traveled best with only Maggot. But then when he thought about it, he knew that he was tired of being alone and that these past weeks with Ophelia had been the happiest of his long and mostly lonesome life.

"We can try it out," he said. "We can see how we get along."

Ophelia hugged her grandfather and knew that, if she could somehow avoid shooting that horrible white mule, she and Bruin Henry would get along just fine.

WOLF MACKENNA

THE BURNING TRAIL
0-425-18694-6
"COMPELLING WESTERN WITH FAST ACTION
AND ENGAGING CHARACTERS."
—PETER BRANDVOLD

DUST RIDERS
0-425-17698-3
A VENGEFUL COWBOY AND A TENDERFOOT YANKEE
JOIN FORCES TO TRACK MURDEROUS THIEVES
THROUGH TERRAIN THAT'S EQUALLY DEADLY.

GUNNING FOR REGRET
0-425-17880-3
SHERIFF DIX GRANGER AND HIS PRISONER FIND
THEMSELVES IN THE TOWN OF REGRET, WAITING OUT A
STORM. WHEN ONE OF THE TOWN'S RESIDENTS
KILLS AN APACHE, DIX KNOWS IT'S UP TO HIM TO
DEFEND THE TOWN FROM APACHE VENGEANCE.

B134